"Bella?"

Cal's eyes had turned steely gray. "I've been standing here in the dark watching the plain because I can feel those *coyotes* out there… somewhere. I'm afraid I've made a mistake bringing you out here."

Bella looked out through the window into the black night. "Have you seen something?"

He reached up and took hold of her shoulders. "No. But I don't need that to know they're out there." He squeezed her shoulders, as if to push her away. Instead his fingers massaged…caressed. Aroused beyond belief, he said, "Go to bed."

But his hands stayed where they were. Too close. Too intimate.

Bella threw her arms around his neck. "Take me there."

Staggered, his blood was racing. He leaned against the kitchen counter to keep himself steady. But he didn't have a chance to think about it.

"Take me," she whispered in his ear. "I know you want me. Take me now."

Dear Reader,

Experience passion and power in six brand-new, provocative titles from Silhouette Desire this July!

Begin with *Scenes of Passion* (#1519) by *New York Times* bestselling author Suzanne Brockmann. In this scintillating love story, a pretend marriage turned all too real reveals the torrid emotions and secrets of a former bad-boy millionaire and his prim heiress.

DYNASTIES: THE BARONES continues in July with *Cinderella's Millionaire* (#1520) by Katherine Garbera, in which a pretty pastry cook's red-hot passion melts the defenses of a brooding Barone hero. *In Bed with the Enemy,* (#1521) by rising star Kathie DeNosky, is the second LONE STAR COUNTRY CLUB title in Desire. In this installment, a lady agent and her lone-wolf counterpart bump more than heads during an investigation into a gun-smuggling ring.

What would you do if you were *Expecting the Cowboy's Baby* (#1522)? Discover how a plain-Jane bookkeeper deals with this dilemma in this steamy love story, the second Silhouette Desire title by popular Harlequin Historicals author Charlene Sands. Then see how a brokenhearted rancher struggles to forgive the woman who betrayed him, in *Cherokee Dad* (#1523) by Sheri WhiteFeather. And in *The Gentrys: Cal* (#1524) by Linda Conrad, a wounded stock-car driver finds healing love in the arms of a sexy, mysterious nurse, and the Gentry siblings at last learn the truth about their parents' disappearance.

Beat the summer heat with these six new love stories from Silhouette Desire.

Enjoy!

Melissa Jeglinski
Senior Editor, Silhouette Desire

Please address questions and book requests to:
Silhouette Reader Service
U.S.: 3010 Walden Ave., P.O. Box 1325, Buffalo, NY 14269
Canadian: P.O. Box 609, Fort Erie, Ont. L2A 5X3

The Gentrys: Cal
LINDA CONRAD

Silhouette® Desire

Published by Silhouette Books

America's Publisher of Contemporary Romance

SILHOUETTE BOOKS

ISBN 0-373-76524-X

THE GENTRYS: CAL

Books by Linda Conrad

LINDA CONRAD

Born in Brazil to a commercial pilot and his wife, Linda Conrad was raised in south Florida and has been a dreamer and storyteller for as long as she can remember. After her mother's death a few years ago, she moved from her then-home in Texas to Southern California and gave up her previous life as a stockbroker to rededicate herself to her first love—writing.

Linda and her husband, along with a Siamese-mix cat named Sam, recently moved back to south Florida. She's been writing contemporary romances for about five years and loves sharing them with readers. She enjoys growing roses, reading cozy mysteries and sexy romances, and driving her little convertible in the sunshine. But most important, Linda loves learning about— and living with—passion.

It makes Linda's day to hear from readers. Visit with her at www.LindaConrad.com.

For Laurie Jayne (with a *y*)
You have my love. My respect for everything you face
with grace and kindness. And my many thanks for
becoming a wonderful adult and a terrific parent.
In my whole life, you have been the best gift
I ever received. I cherish you.

News Flash: Local Celebrity
Involved in Fatal Accident

Gentry Wells native, Callan A. Gentry, suffered critical injuries last week when a pickup trying to evade Fort Worth police sideswiped his van. Gentry's wife, Jasmine, and the driver of the pickup were killed in the accident. Gentry's daughter, four-month-old Kaydie Ann, escaped injury.

A world-renowned stock-car racer and winner of several titles, Gentry inherited a partial ownership in the family ranch twelve years ago after his parents disappeared at sea and were presumed drowned. Gentry graduated from Gentry Wells High School and went on to attend the University of Texas in Austin.

Gentry's condition continues to be listed as serious. A spokesperson for Harris Methodist Hospital in Fort Worth declined to confirm or deny rumors that he will face permanent disability. Speculation from sports media sources has centered on the possibility that Gentry may be forced to abandon plans of returning to the racing circuit next season.

One

Two months later: Gentry Ranch, Texas

No doubt about it. Cal Gentry had finally found something he couldn't handle. He was in way over his head.

He cringed once again at the baby's wail and wondered why on earth his daughter wouldn't stop crying? Holding her loosely in one arm, Cal contemplated his options. With his movements restricted by having to use a crutch for a bum knee, the choices were quickly disintegrating.

Cal jiggled the tiny screaming bundle once more and limped back and forth across the front room of the cabin they were temporarily calling home. The solution to quieting his child seemed more elusive than ever, and his head hurt from worrying about her. Soon he would probably drown in her tears.

He cursed his rotten luck. First, at losing the baby's new nanny this morning—as she'd been the one person who seemed able to settle the child down when she was fretting. And second, because the family's attorney in Gentry Wells, Ray Adler, had been sympathetic but didn't offer much hope for a quick fix. And Cal needed a solution—now.

A loud knock suddenly came from the front door and Cal grimaced. It had to be one of his family come to check on their welfare. Dang, but he hated to look so incompetent and foolish in front of them, almost as much as he hated to go to the main ranch house and face the sad memories and his own glaring lack of independence.

The knocking grew more insistent and a bright new thought occurred to him. What if Ray had been wrong and it had only taken a few hours to locate a replacement for Mrs. Garcia?

Cal inched toward the front door as fast as his useless leg would let him. When he got there, it took a minute to lean the crutch against the wall, shift his weight so he could stand alone, and rearrange the baby to ensure she wouldn't squirm out of his grip. As he accomplished it all, the thought that the person knocking must be someone sent to be the baby's nanny became more and more plausible in his mind. He eagerly threw open the door.

Before him stood one of the most exotic and beautiful women he'd ever beheld. Cal couldn't help the gasp that escaped his lips.

After he'd swallowed a couple of times and managed a second look, he realized that the gorgeous Mexican-American woman on the doorstep also appeared somewhat haggard. In her mid-twenties, she appeared to be a little older than his sister. The worse-for-the-wear clothes she wore hung loosely on her ultra-thin frame. Her shoes were filthy, dust and mud clung to them like she'd walked both through shallow puddles and the deep Texas dirt.

Aside from her weary-traveler appearance, she was downright spectacular. Warm-chocolate eyes with golden highlights stared out of a perfect heart-shaped face. Her expression was laced with a kind of soul-searching starkness.

But her skin, the color of golden honey, looked as smooth as a brand-new fiberglass paint job. She'd pulled back her long, shiny black hair into an untidy ponytail. The strands resembled spun silk where they flew loose around her face.

"¿Señor? I saw the smoke from your chimney. Excuse the interruption but…"

The musical sound of her voice rising above the baby's cries broke into Cal's stupor.

"Thank God you've come!" he shouted at her over the din. "Come in. Hurry!"

Snatching up his crutch again, he shuffled aside to allow her to enter. She hesitated and looked at him with a puzzled expression, but finally began to step inside.

When she'd taken only a few tentative movements to cross the threshold, those beautiful limpid eyes focused on Kaydie. "What is wrong with the little one?" she asked.

"Wrong? I have no idea. I don't know what she wants. I can't make her stop screaming." He shoved the baby in her direction. "Here, you see what you can do."

Suddenly the extraordinary eyes he'd been concentrating his whole attention upon flashed angrily. "You do not treat a baby in that way," she fiercely announced.

"It's not my fault," Cal began as he released his child into the woman's arms. "I am not equipped…"

Immediately she cradled Kaydie in her arms and placed a soft kiss against her forehead. *"Madre de Dios!"* she exclaimed, interrupting his excuses. *"Pobrecita.* This child is *muy caliente."*

Cal thought that meant that Kaydie felt hot. But he wasn't sure, and all he really wanted was to make her screaming come to an end. "Will kissing her make her stop that squalling?"

"Do you know nothing about children?" the woman muttered. "Putting my lips to her hot skin tells me this baby is burning up with fever. And you do nothing for her but complain about the crying?" Her gorgeous brown eyes were shooting sparks of anger in his direction.

"Hey. That's not fair. I'm not—"

"Have you called her doctor?"

Cal shook his head. "We just moved here, and she was fine this morning."

"And she is what…six months old?"

"Yes, almost, but—"

"Where is the kitchen?"

Cal pointed toward the back of the cabin.

"We shall see what we can do," she said, and rushed off carrying the baby in her arms.

Cal stood at the open front door and stared after her. What had just happened here? The strange but spectacular-looking woman wasn't dressed like any nanny he'd ever seen, and she'd never actually said she was a nanny, either.

It suddenly occurred to him that he'd just handed

over his daughter to a total stranger. He stepped out to look around the cabin's empty yard and began to wonder who this rather prickly and hotheaded woman might really be.

And who had brought her all the way out here? Come to think of it, Cal hadn't heard any noises at all that might've been her transportation.

This morning he'd given Mrs. Garcia the keys to his Suburban when she'd demanded to be returned to civilization, and told her to just leave the truck at the bus station in Gentry Wells. The doctors wouldn't let him drive yet, anyway, and Cal knew it would only take a phone call to his older brother, Cinco, to get transportation or supplies to them whenever necessary. So the cabin's yard stood completely empty of vehicles.

But how did this stranger get her things out here if she came any other way? He looked around the front stairs and found one bundle that looked like rags tied together. The woman had obviously hidden it under some bushes.

Hmm. This definitely was not adding up.

She could be an escaped convict or a lunatic or any of a dozen unsavory characters. He'd handed over his tiny daughter to an exotic woman who just might be a crazed maniac. What was the matter with him? Had he been so mesmerized by a pretty face that he'd totally lost his mind?

Where were her references? How did she get here? His brain finally began working once again. He hadn't even asked the most basic of questions. Like what the heck was her name?

He steadied himself with his crutch and, following the sound of his daughter's cries, he limped toward the kitchen—and some answers.

* * *

Bella Fernandez fought back her irritation at the gringo's lack of sympathy for the sick baby girl. She'd come begging for a little help and compassion for herself. But when she'd seen his seeming ignorance and confusion over the helpless child, righteous indignation got the best of her.

That had always been one of her worst faults, she sighed. Stepping in and opening her mouth when she should've kept her thoughts and opinions to herself. The current turmoil bringing her to this remote cabin in the United States stemmed from just that same sort of thing.

She gently laid the baby on the kitchen counter and removed the little girl's dress and diaper. Murmuring to the child as she went, Bella quickly checked her over for any signs that this might be more than a simple childhood fever.

The baby wasn't convulsing and had no skin lesions, rashes or contusions. She didn't seem dehydrated. Her tears were falling easily, her lips weren't dry or cracked. No yellow appeared in her eyes and she certainly wasn't excessively lethargic or sleepy.

The swinging kitchen door opened up behind her. "What are you doing to my child?"

In the bright golden light of the late-afternoon sun streaming through the kitchen window, Bella noticed for the first time what the confused man really looked like. Early thirties, lean but broad-shouldered, his light-brown hair was cut short in back yet hung down over his forehead. Bella felt a crude rush of awakening but wished she hadn't.

Instead of answering his question right away, she continued examining the baby and studying the man at the same time. She could tell a ladies' man from miles away, and this one was most certainly qualified. His sharp, gray-green eyes focused intently on her. But those eyes also held an underlying potent sexual draw.

To complete the perfectly dashing picture, full lips and a cleft in his chin softened what would otherwise be a too severely chiseled jaw. That erotic magnetism in his eyes made him look rather devil-may-care and young.

All in all, his looks succeeded in showing off a thrilling mixture of allure put together with a rock-hard promise of passion. She turned her back to him and concentrated her attentions on the baby.

Yes, most women would definitely fall under the spell of this charmer. Good thing she wasn't most women.

Bella's first lesson about charming men came from trying to get the attention of the dashing man who was her father. After she grew up, she became engaged to another charmer—and that one really brought home the point.

Given a choice, she'd rather stay a hundred miles away from an attractive and lady-pleasing man like this gringo, but right now she saw no other alternative. She would not leave a sick child, no matter what.

Without turning around, she finally asked a couple of questions of her own. "Do you have a flashlight and a baby thermometer?"

"What? Why?" He came close and looked over her shoulder. "What's wrong with Kaydie?"

"I told you, she has a fever. I'm trying to determine why and how bad it might be." Bella never looked up at him, though she could feel his body's warmth seeping through her thin clothes, making her wonder if she might be running a fever, too. "Where is the child's mother?"

A long, deadly silence followed her question, and Bella realized the baby had quieted down.

"My wife, Kaydie's mother, was killed in a car accident a couple of months ago." His voice was so hushed, Bella could barely make out the words.

He laid a firm hand on Bella's shoulder. "Who are you?"

Keeping both hands on the baby's warm body, Bella turned her head to answer him. "I'm sorry for your recent loss, *señor*. My name is Isabella Maria Fernandez. But please call me Bella." She managed a half smile, trying to ignore the brushfire he'd ignited inside her with his touch. "Can we have our discussions later? Right now your daughter's welfare should be your first concern."

"She *is* my first concern." His fingers dug lightly into her shoulder. "Where are you from, Bella? Who sent you?"

"No one sent me." Did this man not realize how potentially serious a high fever could be? "Please. I will tell you everything just as soon as I am satisfied the baby is not in immediate danger."

"What do you know about this kind of thing? Do you have children of your own, or are you a doctor?"

His hold on her shoulder tightened, and she winced involuntarily. "In my country I am a licensed nurse. I received training in the United States to be what you call a *practical* nurse." She tried to twist free of his grip. "*Por favor,* you're hurting me. Let me do what I can for your daughter. Then we will talk."

He eased his hand from her shoulder, but his six-foot frame towered over them as he continued to keep a steady watch on his daughter. Bella thought he must truly be concerned and aware of his duty to his own flesh and blood, but he didn't seem to know the first thing about how to care for a sick child.

"Do you have a flashlight and a baby thermometer?" she repeated.

"I saw a flashlight in this drawer." He pulled open a cabinet drawer and handed her the heavy metal light. "There may be a thermometer in Kaydie's things in the front room. I haven't had a chance to unpack yet."

He hesitated while Bella coaxed the baby to open her mouth. With one free hand she held the child's head and with the other Bella pointed the light down her throat.

The father looked as if he wanted to pace the floor, but his obvious leg injuries held him back. "I'll go look through her things for a thermometer. I think the boxes are marked." He took his crutch and began to limp toward the doorway but turned before he'd gone through. "Will she be all right?"

"Yes. Your daughter should be okay. Her throat looks fine and she doesn't seem to be in as much distress as she was when I arrived. Let's just take her temperature to be sure, though. Okay?"

The *norteamericano* father nodded once then disappeared on his mission.

"Ah, *niña*," Bella cooed to the child. "What are you doing way out here with a man who can barely help himself, let alone take care of a baby? Why is there no woman to attend to you?"

Bella had been struck by the lack of emotion in the gringo's voice when he'd mentioned his wife's death. Perhaps he was still so grief-stricken that he dared not even speak of her in case he broke down. Bella knew lots of men in Mexico who would act in that same way. She vowed not to mention the baby's mother again unless he brought her up first.

Bella felt sure that the fever had already lessened its grip on the child's body. "Kaydie, wasn't it?" The baby's light-blue eyes stared up at her in that curious way some babies had. "Well, Kaydie. Let's see if we can make you a little more comfortable."

After turning on the water tap, Bella waited a few minutes for the water to reach the right lukewarm temperature. Carefully she placed the baby in the sink, but not directly under the water's stream. Cupping her hand, she put a bit of the water on the baby's chest and tummy, then let the water fill the sink.

"How does that feel?" she asked in Spanish.

Kaydie responded by widening her eyes and hiccuping. She seemed to understand the language—or perhaps it was the tone that Bella used. Or maybe the baby just liked the feel of the tepid water on her heated skin. Bella turned off the water faucet and held the baby in the sink while the water turned colder.

"Are you giving her a bath?" The father's voice startled Bella as he dragged himself back into the room. "I found a thermometer, and I brought her diaper bag."

"Good.. Set the bag down on the table, then come here and hold Kaydie while I take her temperature."

"Yes, ma'am," he grumbled while he did as she'd asked.

Bella knew a disgruntled tone when she heard one, but she didn't care. He had an air about him that, like many *norteamericano* men, said he was powerful, rich and accustomed to getting things done his own way.

But right now he needed her help. And he could darn well do things *her* way to get it.

She dried Kaydie off and wrapped her in a clean towel. Instructing the child's father to sit, she placed her in his lap. While he held the baby, Bella stuck the digital thermometer in her ear to take her temperature.

"You know my name, *señor*," she asked as she held the thermometer in place. "May I ask for yours?"

"Gentry," the man bristled.

When Bella continued to watch him expectantly, this Gentry fellow seemed to realize he had more of a name than just that.

"Cal Gentry."

Bella shrugged a shoulder. A nice name, she thought. But not one she'd ever heard before. Cal had said it as though she should definitely be impressed. She wasn't.

"Well, Cal, your daughter's temperature must have subsided with the cool bath. This thermometer says 101 degrees." Bella put aside the thermometer and lifted the baby back into her arms. "Does she have a change of clothes in that bag you brought?"

"I guess so." He picked up the bag and scooted it over the tabletop toward her. "I think I saw some clothes in there. But I didn't pack it, so I'm not positive."

She could've guessed that this father would be unsure about his daughter's care. When Bella had first held her, the baby's pink dress was buttoned backward and the tabs on her plastic diapers dangled dangerously below it.

She held Kaydie against her left shoulder. With her other hand, Bella rummaged through the duffle. She found powder, creams and antibiotic wipes in one of the side pockets. Inside the main compartment were several changes of clothes, plastic diapers and a few small bottles filled with juice and water. Another pocket revealed baby-strength liquid aspirin substitute, vitamins, a few bottles of rehydration fluid and jars of processed baby food.

What Bella wouldn't have given for such a fantastic stash when she'd worked with the small bands of Mexican families on the border. She'd been making do with whatever was handy for so long that she almost didn't recognize some of the things.

Jealousy and curiosity got the best of her. "If you didn't pack this bag, then who did?" she finally asked.

He scrunched up his mouth and rolled his eyes. "I guess I made a big mistake. I was so anxious to make a fresh start and come back to the old family homestead that I hired the first nanny I could find who would agree to leave Fort Worth.

"The woman hadn't learned to like Kaydie yet, as she'd only been with us a couple of days. So when she got a good look at the place in the sunlight, she threw her hands up and claimed the cabin was falling down and not safe."

"She left you and the baby alone here?" Bella was stunned. What kind of woman would do such a thing?

"Yeah. I told her to go. There's absolutely nothing the matter with this old place. I think it looks great. If I can manage to get some temporary help with the baby, I'll do just fine here."

An hour later Cal was still wondering who this absolutely beautiful and sensual woman was and why the heck she'd apparently been wandering around on the Gentry Ranch alone. It just didn't add up.

She'd been busy, giving Kaydie some of the children's Tylenol after the bath. Then she'd dressed the baby up in soft nightclothes, still too busy to adequately answer his questions. But she seemed to know exactly what she was doing with a sick baby, so he shut up and let her attend to things.

Cal peeked into the little room off the kitchen that he'd planned to make into the nanny's bedroom and where he'd set up Kaydie's things last night. Bella bent over the crib, laying a soft baby blanket lightly across Kaydie's feet.

After she'd finished, she sat down on the single bed by the baby's portable crib, watching Kaydie sleep as the dim shadows of twilight darkened the room.

"Is she better?" he whispered.

Bella got up and crept toward him as he stood in the doorway. "*Sí.* The fever has subsided."

He backed away to let her come into the kitchen.

The minute she'd partially closed the door behind her, Bella drew a deep breath. "I think perhaps Kaydie's father also needs his sleep. You look as though it's been a very rough day, *señor.* I noticed the bed in the baby's room. You'd better sleep there tonight in case she needs you."

She sighed and tried to stifle an obvious yawn. "If I may be permitted some water for my journey and perhaps a few directions to the border, I should be on my way."

"You're leaving?" That thought hadn't occurred to him.

In fact, Cal had been quite relieved to think she would be here all night in case Kaydie awoke in trouble. And besides, they still needed to talk. He wanted to find out all about her. He wanted to talk to her. Tomorrow. When he could get a better grip on things.

Couldn't she see he and Kaydie needed help? But more than that, couldn't she feel the same draw he felt when he looked at her? There was something… something…

Well, maybe it was just lust, but it felt deeper, more fundamental somehow. Cal was not about to let her out of here until he had a chance to explore what was happening between them.

Tired and irritable, he knew he couldn't cope with Kaydie any more tonight, either. Tomorrow, after a good night's sleep, everything would seem easier and clearer.

"You cannot leave tonight. You'll sleep here," he commanded. "I'll bring your things."

Two

"Me perdona?" Bella questioned Cal's words in a deliberately hushed voice because she didn't want to wake the baby.

But she also narrowed her eyes at the demanding and arrogant gringo. Perhaps her English was rustier than she'd thought. Certainly, he had not just commanded her to sleep with him.

Because she was so tired, Bella felt sure her ears had played tricks on her. He'd simply meant that she spend the night, nothing more sinister than that. Obviously her hunger was playing games with her mind.

Still, she knew an order when she heard one. Whether he'd been demanding that she sleep with him or ordering her to spend the night for safety's sake, he was in for a fight.

She lifted her chin in defiance, but her empty stomach betrayed her. Its rumbling complaint could be heard throughout the house. She folded her arms across her waist and tightly held herself together in the middle.

If she remained still, maybe Cal would ignore the noisy reminder that she hadn't eaten. He might even help her to be on her way. She was still worried that the men who chased her would be closing in, so she needed to leave this cabin and find a place to hide soon—before her presence put the baby and her injured father in grave danger.

But no such luck. He'd definitely heard her stomach's grumble. It would've been hard to ignore. The stern and commanding expression on his face melted into a cocky but utterly disarming smile. The jaunty ladies' man was back. Even with his disability, he gave the impression of being strong and virile—yet still tender and giving.

"You are pardoned, sugar. But it's not hard to tell you're hungry. Where are my manners?" He took her elbow with his free hand and gingerly guided them both back into the kitchen. "Let me get you something to eat. And I'll make us some coffee."

Bella allowed him to lead her back to the kitchen table. To tell the truth, the weakness from hunger had already begun to show up in her lack of stamina and the silly wanderings of her mind. But she was grateful for his charity. She knew she wouldn't have lasted much longer.

She'd decided to accept his hospitality, but also made the decision that he would not make demands on her just because she was a woman alone in the wilderness. If she chose to stay for the night, it would be because she wanted a safe place to sleep—not because he'd insisted.

All these months on the open range, working with families of migrants, had taught her to watch out for herself. She would not be coerced by force—or by charm.

But goodness, when he smiled and that warm glow in his eyes focused on her, the attractive and tempting Cal Gentry was certainly a joy to behold. Not only did he look good enough to eat, his scent drove her to distraction. And his voice washed over her like rich Mexican chocolate. Dark, deep and sensual.

Bella knew he was in pain, she could see the fine lines of it around his eyes, but he still seemed to need to be the host. "I can do this myself," she told him. "I'm a good cook. Just sit and tell me where things are."

"No, thanks. You're my guest, and you helped with the baby. I can handle it." Trying to keep the slight irritation out of his voice, Cal took the water pitcher from the refrigerator and showed Bella where the drinking glasses were kept.

Exceedingly grateful that the kitchen in this cabin was compact and efficient, he knew his disjointed movements might be slow, but he figured he could get the job done with everything so easily accessible. And maybe, with a little coffee, he'd be able to think clearly enough to ask a couple of his questions.

While he brewed coffee, she drank two big glasses of water, then sat down quietly at the tiny table with the yellow-checked plastic cover. He wondered who she really was and what she might have been going through before she showed up at his door. She looked half-starved and exhausted, but her natural beauty and her passion for life shone brilliantly through bright, clear eyes.

"Will you tell me now how you came to be at our door this afternoon, Bella?" He struck a casual pose as he continued fixing her coffee and a sandwich. "What's a practical nurse doing alone on Gentry ranchland?"

When she turned her deep-set, brown eyes to stare up at him, their depths seemed to contain more mysteries than answers. "I did not realize I was on your ranch, *señor*. I have been walking for slightly less than two days, searching for a safe way back across the border to my home."

"The Mexican border? You're a long way from any normal crossing point here." Cal tried to ignore the inexplicable tug in his gut whenever he looked at her. "In fact, we're about 250 miles from Lake Amistad, and that's as close as the Rio Grande comes to the ranch. You're really lost, aren't you?"

She heaved a huge sigh. "*Sí*, I suppose I am. That was the reason I decided to risk stopping here. I was out of choices."

"But how did you get onto the Gentry Ranch? What are you doing walking across the range alone?" The questions poured from his mouth. "And how did you come across the border in the first place?" He set the sandwich he'd made down on the table in front of her and reached above the counter for a couple of coffee mugs for them both.

Before she answered any of his questions, she daintily picked up the turkey sandwich and took a bite. Her eyes closed as she swallowed the food, and the passionate expression on her face looked as if this was the best meal she'd ever eaten. Cal knew his cooking abilities left a lot to be desired and the sandwich fixings had been rather plain in the first place. It was just lunch meat on wheat bread—not ambrosia of the gods.

"How long has it been since you last ate anything?" he inquired.

Bella quickly swallowed two more bites before she answered. "I will answer all your questions, but this is the first food I've eaten in two days. May I finish first?"

"Two days?" The woman was truly starving to death.

Cal wondered if he would be so polite and quiet if he hadn't had anything to eat in forty-eight hours. He took a bowl of fruit off the counter. Placing the apples and bananas on the table in front of her, he sat down and waited, encouraging her to finish every last bite of sandwich.

After she'd washed down the sandwich with the coffee, Bella sighed once more. "Thank you, Cal." She eyed the fruit, but folded her hands in her lap. "I believe it might make me sick to eat too much after such a long time. I will try a banana later…if the sandwich settles well."

She seemed so poised and unhurried. He reached for an apple himself, suddenly feeling ravenous. Man, if it was him who hadn't eaten in that long, he'd be grabbing and stuffing by this time. Just who was this woman, anyway?

Bella took one more sip of coffee as he bit into his apple. "There," she said. "I think I can talk now. I appreciate your hospitality."

He swallowed and reached for her hand with his free one. "It's nothing, Bella. I would've fed you earlier if I'd known. You should've told me."

She shook her head. "The baby came first. It was only right."

Bella looked down at their joined hands. The glow of heat she'd felt when he touched her had been a surprise. She'd thought herself immune to such feelings of lust after all this time on the open range, away from temptation.

"Now then, where to begin?" She considered pulling her hand from under his, but decided to leave it where it was for the moment. "This is the first time that I have actually crossed into your country illegally. I did not realize how far into Texas we'd come."

She knew her words had taken him aback when he quietly removed his hand and took another bite of apple. Bella wondered what he'd say when he learned she was running from such dire circumstances.

"Perhaps I should begin at the beginning and tell you why I have been working in the Mexican countryside near your borders," she said, sighed and then continued. "Several years ago my church in Mexico decided to start a…how do you say it…'missionary outreach.' Is that not right? Anyway, many of our poorer countrymen take huge risks to come to your country. Unfortunately, too many of them also die for their trouble. We wanted to…*I* wanted to…make a difference for a few."

"So you…did what? Went on a hunger strike?" Cal interrupted.

There was that arrogant tone again, even through the disarming grin. The man just oozed sex appeal in his trendy designer jeans and blue-striped western shirt. And his new clothes covered a broad chest narrowing down to perfect slim hips, too. But he couldn't manage to keep his demanding, rich-man's ways hidden for long.

Judging by the look of his expensive clothes and the smug sexual way he stared at her, he appeared to be a man used to getting his own way. She had no doubt that the women around him fawned over him, spoiling him and making him cocksure of himself where it came to the opposite sex.

She wasn't quite sure what he was doing in this cabin that looked a little shabby around the edges, though he'd said it was temporary. But she knew he lived on a big Texas ranch and could afford a nanny for his child. Bella wondered if she should bother explaining anything to this demanding and probably extremely rich charmer.

Since he was her host, she decided to try. "No. For four years the church has sent teams to our border," she began again. "We camp out, eventually finding small bands of migrants heading north. We take them health care and a rudimentary knowledge of how to remain safe during their journey through the wilderness."

"Do you try to talk them out of coming here?" he asked.

Bella shook her head. "It would do no good. Poverty drives them from their homes and spurs them to seek a better way in this land of plenty. Nothing we could say would change their desperation." She wondered whether he would listen to the whole story. "My job is to bring them a little medicine, though I cannot carry everything they need. We talk to them about sanitation, about regulating their body temperatures and staying hydrated." Taking a last sip of coffee, she eyed the fruit bowl.

"That all sounds very noble of you," Cal commented dryly.

She glared at him. "What we do, we do for our countrymen and their families…and for God. Not for glory."

As annoying as his remarks might be, she was glad he'd asked. She'd sort of lost track of the point of it all. Telling him reminded her of the reasons she took this challenge in the first place—to save lives.

Cal took one last bite of apple and spoke after he swallowed. "Yes, well, that doesn't tell me why you're here alone in Texas. Did you decide to come across with some migrants this time?" he asked at last.

He loved the way her eyes sparked as she talked. The fire and enthusiasm for what she was doing flashed out of every pore. She had to be exhausted and near collapse, but she seemed determined to make him understand. He discovered it aroused him no end to simply listen and watch.

He'd slept with a number of women in his youth, but he'd never seen this much pure passion packed into one gorgeous body. Cal experienced a demanding desire to capture that passion. But he also badly needed her help with Kaydie. So he decided to go slow and eventually charm his way into her arms.

"I usually travel with one or two other church members," she told him. "On this particular journey, two of us had been working with one of the bigger migrant groups…Armando with the single men, and I was with the families that had mothers and babies along." Bella rose, refilled her glass.

"Three nights ago the dangerous men who'd promised to take the whole group across the border showed up at the camp." She took a sip and returned to her seat. "Your U.S. law enforcement uses the term *coyotes* for the *hombres* who guide migrants across for money. The name suits most of them and certainly described these men."

Cal began to wonder exactly what details her story might entail. A look of terror had flitted across her eyes as she spoke of the *coyotes*.

"You look tired, Bella." He swallowed back the flash of anger over the treatment he'd imagined she'd suffered at the hands of the human smugglers. "Why don't you finish telling me this tomorrow?" He wasn't sure he could take hearing the details of what had happened to her.

She shook her head. "I will finish now, *por favor*." Bella blinked once and shivered. "The men who were to act as *coyotes* for our band of migrants seemed particularly bad. Rough, drunken and violent. Armando and I talked the women and children into staying inside Mexico and trying to find another way to cross. The single men wanted to go ahead.

"The *coyotes* were displeased with Armando and me for interfering with their plans…and for warning the single men not to turn over all their money until they'd arrived safely at their destination."

Wiping a hand across her weary eyes, Bella suddenly looked vulnerable and small. "A *coyote* shot Armando. Killed him instantly. One of the single migrant men hid me under a tarp in the bed of a covered truck…or I would be dead, too."

Cal reached for her, but she shirked away from his touch. "My God, Bella. This sounds incredible. How did you survive? What did you do?"

"I kept perfectly still while the *coyotes* herded the rest of the migrants into the trucks. It was so hot in there and we had so little air, breathing was difficult. The first time they stopped the trucks to provide for some human comfort must've been nearly twelve hours later.''

Bella closed her eyes, apparently remembering the horror. ''Some of the migrants feared that if the *coyotes* spotted me they might try to assault me and perhaps kill us all. One kind man gave me a little water that he'd hidden and then helped me escape into the night.

''I had no idea how far we had come before I got away…or where I might be headed. But I was panicked that the *coyotes* would come looking for me. They know the Texas range…and they want me dead.'' She took a breath and swallowed. ''I waited until daylight and then traveled south, hoping to run into something recognizable sooner or later.''

Cal stood. He felt like punching something, but there was nothing to hit. So he pitched his apple core into the garbage can and limped to the sink. Her story had disturbed him more than he liked to think.

''How did you manage to get through the Gentry Ranch fence?'' he grumbled over his shoulder.

''Well, I most certainly did not cut any wires to come here, Señor Gentry,'' she retorted smartly. ''The trucks stopped on a dirt road in the dark of night and out in the middle of nowhere. I have no idea how we arrived at that spot, considering that I was buried under a dozen men in the dark trying not to breathe too loudly. I saw no signs of civilization when I snuck away.

''At daybreak, I walked south. I came across cattle and sheep and took water from stock tanks, but I saw no one's fence. The smoke from the chimney of this cabin was the first thing I saw that looked like civilization.''

Upon hearing the obvious annoyance in her words, Cal had swung to watch her face. ''I didn't mean to accuse you of trespassing, sugar.'' He hoped he could take the darts from her gaze with an explanation. ''But my older brother, Cinco, will have a fit when he hears of this. He prides himself on the security surrounding Gentry Ranch.''

Bella's hand motioned around the tiny kitchen. ''Your brother lives here, too? I've only seen one bedroom bedsides Kaydie's little room. Where is your brother now?''

Cal chuckled. ''Most of the time no one lives in this cabin. Kaydie, her nanny and I just arrived last night. The nanny left this morning.'' He sighed, then continued. ''Cinco and his wife live in the main ranch house, about a half hour drive from here.''

At her startled look, he explained. ''The Gentry is a good-size Texas ranch, honey. If you walked south all day yesterday, you must've escaped the *coyotes'* truck about ten or twelve miles *inside* our eastern fence line. The question is how and where the *coyotes* broke through.''

''I didn't realize your ranch was that big. There are rich *patróns* in Mexico who also have such massive land holdings.'' She shrugged a shoulder. ''But I don't know how we arrived on your land in the trucks. We had no windows or way to see out. I did hear the *coyotes* bragging to the migrants about how they'd found a new, perfectly safe way to travel north, though.''

When she finished speaking, she yawned again, and Cal instinctively wanted to cradle her in his arms and rock her until she relaxed enough to fall sleep. He was surprised at the protective feelings she'd suddenly aroused in him. They felt a lot like the fatherly urges toward Kaydie he'd been trying to ignore for the last couple of months.

He couldn't afford to suddenly feel anything more than duty when it came to his child. Not now. And with Bella…well, with her he wanted to keep his urges running more toward the lustful side anyway.

"You need sleep," he told her.

He noticed her studying him carefully so he explained. "I want you to stay with us…at least for tonight. Tomorrow I'll make some calls and we'll talk more about getting you home. You can't just wander around on the Gentry Ranch, starving and in danger of sunstroke."

She gestured toward his gimpy leg. "Will someone come to care for Kaydie tonight? Forgive me, Cal, but you are not in very good shape to care for such a small and sick child."

"You're telling me," he said with a nod. "No. No one else will be coming here tonight. It's just my daughter and me. Kaydie has had one nursemaid or another since she was born, but the one I hired to come out here felt the place was too…rustic…for her tastes."

Bella looked around the kitchen. "Running water. Indoor plumbing. Two bedrooms with safe and cozy beds in which to sleep." She smiled. "This place would be a palace to some. How long has this cabin been here?"

For the first time since she'd known him, Cal smiled with real pleasure. "My great-great-grandfather built it by hand for one of his children over a hundred years ago. I figure it's sturdy enough to still be standing here for at least another hundred.

"My sister and I used to play in these old rooms as kids," he continued. "Abby…that's my little sister…and her new husband, Gray, moved in right after they got married and started remodeling the old place. They rewired and put in new plumbing. In fact, they really brought the cabin up to date…except for a few cosmetic problems. They stopped and moved out when Gray's stepfather died, but I plan on fixing up the rest of it while I'm here."

"How long will you and Kaydie live out here?"

"I'm thinking we'll probably stay a couple of months…. It all depends."

Bella looked around the warm and safe cabin once more. She knew the *coyotes* might be looking for her, now that it was dark again. And at some point she would have to start worrying about the U.S. Border Patrol catching her and carting her off to a detention cell, then hustling her off across the border.

It didn't take her long to figure out her best plan would be to stay here, acting as the sweet baby's nanny. Maybe she could also help the child's injured father—even though being near to Cal made her feel lots of things that she shouldn't.

"I will stay with you tonight," she told him. "But only for the baby's sake. And only…if I sleep alone in the little bed next to her crib."

Bella awoke with a start. As she lay perfectly still and held her breath, she listened carefully for the sound or movement that must've disturbed her sleep. Had the *coyotes* found her?

A small, soft noise in the baby's crib next to her bed

suddenly reminded her of where she was and how she'd gotten here. Before sitting up and trying to clear the rest of the ravages of sleep from her brain, she took a second to think about how fantastic a real mattress and box springs felt after all these months of sleeping on the ground.

When the last speck of the dark *coyote* nightmare that had been plaguing her for days finally cleared away, she rose to check on the baby.

The child was on her back with her eyes closed, but she seemed restless. Bella reached to check her diaper, thinking perhaps the girl was wet and uncomfortable. But the moment her hand touched the baby's sizzling skin, Bella knew what was really wrong. Kaydie's fever had come back.

Bella quickly changed the diaper then cradled the child to her chest. The baby snuggled close, trying to find comfort against a women's breast. But after a fruitless minute, Kaydie pushed herself back and began to wail.

"Ah, *pobrecita.* You do not feel well, I know," Bella cooed. "Let's see if we can find a way to help."

With Kaydie still crying, Bella headed toward the darkened kitchen and the baby bottles she'd washed out earlier. "We'll get you some water and check you over again, little one," she told the screaming child.

Not sure where the light switch might be, and with the cool moonlight streaming through the windows, Bella didn't bother with the lights. There was enough of a glow for her to fill a baby bottle. After all, she'd become accustomed to maneuvering in the dark over the last couple of years on the open range.

But as she reached the counter and shifted Kaydie enough to pick up a bottle, the overhead light suddenly flooded the room with a shock of glaring illumination. Bella turned to make sure the interloper was Cal.

It was most definitely, absolutely positively, her host.

He stood motionless, leaning on one crutch at the threshold of the kitchen, scrutinizing her. He looked like he'd just stumbled out of bed. His hair was in luxuriant disarray, the deep shadow of a late-night beard grazed across his jaw, and he was wearing only a pair of loose fitting running shorts. His naked broad chest and the smattering of dark hair there caught her immediate attention—until she glanced into his eyes.

As his gaze raked her body, from the tip of her uncombed hair right down to her bare toes, a spark of sexual recognition hammered through every single part of her. Burning passion flamed openly in his eyes as he brought his gaze up to meet hers.

She had to clear her throat twice to speak. "You did not need to get up. I told you I would take care of Kaydie."

The man was every sexual fantasy she'd ever had all wrapped into one package. She wondered if he'd be tender or rough, whether he'd try to please her or continue with his selfish ways in bed. Hmm.

She shook off the images. It didn't matter. She didn't even know him. She vowed there would be no fantasies with Cal, sexual or otherwise.

"I…" Cal was almost rendered speechless by the sight of the sleep-tousled, golden-skinned woman in bare feet. The sexy dark-haired angel, standing next to the kitchen sink, cradled his child to her breast.

He could not for the life of him figure out why that vision seemed so erotic. Never once, while he'd been married to the baby's mother, had he ever felt anything even resembling passion when his wife had held their child—which really hadn't been too often, come to think of it. And he'd even read that fathers-to-be were sometimes filled with great passion toward their wives when they were expecting—but he'd had good reason *not* to be.

When his eyes met Bella's just now, he not only felt more turned on than he could remember, but he also recognized that same inexplicably tender tug deep in his gut that he'd noticed earlier. He didn't know what that was all about, or why it had hit him so suddenly, but he certainly had no intention of exploring the feeling at the moment. He swallowed hard a couple of times, trying to dislodge the pull from his craw.

"Sorry to startle you, babe." He tried one of his fail-proof smiles. "I heard Kaydie's cries and thought maybe you might need help."

She rolled her eyes. With a look that said, "A lot of good you'd be with your leg slowing you down," she turned back to the baby.

Cal couldn't imagine why Bella didn't react to his smiles the same way other women did. But, so help him, he intended to make it a point to charm his way into her good graces—and maybe a whole lot more. It seemed like kind of a challenge now. But he had to be careful not to rush things and scare her off.

He moved closer while Bella fumbled with a baby bottle and the bottled water. "Here. Let me," he offered.

She relinquished the bottle and rearranged Kaydie in her arms. "I think the fever is back. But not so bad as before." She laid her cheek against the baby's forehead. "Yes, she's cooler. But there's something else…"

Three

Cal handed Bella the bottle, but his expression remained alert. "What else?"

She put the bottle's nipple into Kaydie's mouth, but the baby didn't seem to want to take it. "Ah, *sí,*" Bella said. "It is as I thought. Your daughter has a cold, *señor.* Her nose is stuffy and she's having trouble breathing."

"Is there anything we can do for her?" His eyes had filled with concern.

"I can think of a couple of things that might help," she explained. "Do you have a humidifier?"

He shook his head. "I don't exactly know what that is, but I didn't see anything I couldn't identify when I unpacked the car. Is it important?"

"I think we can manage another way," Bella told him. "But first, will you bring her diaper bag to me, please? I saw something in there that may be of use."

Cal limped toward the front room while she tried to comfort Kaydie. "Shush…shush, *niña*," she crooned. "Your daddy might not know what to do with you, but he obviously cares. Some of us have not been so lucky in our lives."

After Cal returned with the diaper bag, Bella cleaned out the baby's nose the best she could and then found a small jar full of eucalyptus cream. She rubbed some on the baby's chest. Then she and Cal dragged the lightweight crib from the small bedroom into the kitchen.

As he placed it where Bella directed, Cal asked, "Tell me again why she has to sleep in the kitchen?"

"She needs warm moist air. Without a humidifier we can boil water on the stove while she sleeps, and she'll breath easier," Bella replied.

"But won't that mean we'll have to stay with her? It could be dangerous to leave a pot on the stove."

Bella nearly chuckled at the innocence of the man. "*Sí.* I will sit with her and make sure all is well. You may go back to sleep without worry."

"That doesn't seem right," Cal fussed. "You are the one who needs rest. I'll sit up with her. You go on back to bed."

Ah-ha. The charming gringo did have some unselfish thoughts inside him after all. Bella looked beyond the bare chest and broad shoulders that had so far been the focus of her attention and studied Cal's demeanor. She came to the decision that he did have the potential to become the friend she desperately needed.

"We will both sit up with her," she told him. "It is only a few hours before dawn, we could keep each other awake. We may be able to take a nap tomorrow while Kaydie sleeps."

*   *   *

Cal used one hand to push the two-person kitchen table around so both of them would be facing Kaydie's fold-away crib. He couldn't imagine how Bella could remain this alert and wide-awake after everything she'd been through the past few days, but he was grateful for a chance to talk to her.

He still wanted to find a way to get her to like him— at least a little. He was on a mission to keep her here, helping with Kaydie. And maybe even helping him to understand why she affected him the way she did.

Cal pulled out a chair and sat down, watching her settle the baby and then put water on the stove to boil. It took him a minute to notice what she had on.

"Why are you still wearing those same clothes?" He grinned at her.

She looked down at her ripped jeans and dirty long-sleeved shirt. "Oh. I don't have any other clothes with me. I didn't exactly get a chance to pack before I hid in that truck. I'll wash these out tomorrow."

"I know you took a shower before we went to bed…so…you put your dirty clothes back on?" He shook his head. "You can't sleep in jeans," he declared.

"When one is tired enough," she replied as she headed toward her chair, "one can sleep in whatever they happen to be wearing…or in nothing at all for that matter."

Oh, man. He certainly wished she hadn't said that. The image of her lying naked on his cool cotton sheets, waiting for him grabbed him in the gut. How could he be charming when he couldn't even think anymore?

He huffed out a pent-up breath and bit down on the inside of his cheek, trying to make the visions disappear and his errant body behave so he could speak. "I can lend you some T-shirts and sweats to sleep in," he finally managed.

She shook her head. "Oh, I could not—"

"Sure you can. It's no problem for me."

"I suppose that might be better than wearing these old clothes until I can purchase new ones." She gestured to the holes in her pants.

Cal needed to get her talking about something else. Something that would take his mind off the softness of her skin or the silkiness of her thick, dark hair. And off the picture now forming in his head of her in a thigh-topping T-shirt with nothing underneath.

Fortunately, Bella found a good topic—him.

"You said you just arrived here last night," she began as she settled into a chair. "Why have you come to this place, Cal? What business brings you so far away from the main ranch?"

He tapped his injured leg. "A car accident." He smiled wryly. "Which is damn funny considering that I race stock cars for a living."

"What is so funny?"

"I wasn't racing at the time," he muttered as he rearranged his body in a more comfortable position at the table. "You've really never heard of me, honey?" he drawled smoothly. He scrutinized her face, waiting for some kind of reaction.

Surely she'd been putting him on. Everybody knew what had happened to racing giant Cal Gentry.

Her eyebrows rose, but she sat quietly.

"It was in all the papers."

"I don't read newspapers much." Bella shifted in her seat the same way he had. "It's hard to get delivery in places with no roads." She'd said it with a straight face, but her eyes danced with mischievous lights.

Cal could scarcely believe it. She'd made a joke. He'd been convinced that, as erotic as he might find her, she was all commitment and deadly serious. His efforts to charm Bella might just turn out to be fun after all.

His blood began to stir again, liquefying his brain. He fought the sexual urges. But he was sure she would want him as much as he wanted her—sooner or later. He'd never met a woman yet that he couldn't charm into his bed. It was just a matter of time.

"Well, if you'd read any newspapers or magazines, you'd know that I had a reputation as the most expert driver on the circuit. The lucky one who'd never caused a crash." He laughed at the memory of his own foolish pride and stood.

It had suddenly occurred to him that he wanted to see what it would take to shake Bella's composure. He'd had some extremely sensual ideas involving that very thing earlier. But at this moment he just wanted to see her taken aback some—without scaring her off in the process. Underneath her calm exterior lay a hot-blooded woman, and Cal wanted a small preview of what awaited him.

"But that was before I smashed the family minivan into a truck," he continued with a drawl. "A crazy crash on a public freeway managed to put me into the hospital and to kill Kaydie's mother...my wife." He turned away to go and retrieve something for Bella to wear, but added over his shoulder, "You've hooked up with a murderer, sweetheart. How's that for stepping out of a hot spot and into a fire?"

Bella sat poised in silence. Cal thought she was hot
as ice. But a cold flame burned intensely in her eyes.

She showed no reaction to his words, amazing Cal
enough to stop him where he stood. Hadn't she heard
him? He was positive there were fiery passions just
below the surface of her serene outer shell. He'd seen
the signs of it before in her eyes and had been more
than a little intrigued.

But he guessed it didn't take her long to figure out
that he'd been testing her. "I see," she calmly said.
"That is a shame."

The words were spoken in such a deadpan way that
Cal grew irritated at her serene demeanor, even knowing that she was deliberately teasing him in return for
his obnoxious behavior. "Doesn't it bother you that
you're sitting in the same house with a murderer?" he
probed.

Bella let herself smile at the odd gringo. "I am not
totally ignorant of U.S. laws, *señor*. I went to nursing
school in Houston. If you were truly at fault, you would
be facing charges somewhere." He was quite the ex-
aminer, this injured race-car driver, but she knew she
could hold up under his scrutiny. "I'm not some silly
young girl who will believe everything you tell me and
then fall all over one of your smiles."

He scrunched up his forehead and frowned. "Well,
it's true the police didn't charge me…but I was at fault
just the same." Cal looked frustrated and tired. "If
you'll excuse me, I'll go get you those sweats to wear.
I'll be right back."

She had seen by the barely hidden anguish in his
eyes that he did feel guilt for something. When he came
back carrying the clothes, she decided to ask more

about it—even if it just seemed like she was being nosy.

"Please tell me what happened," she asked, and at the same time took the bundle from his arms.

Cal sat back down and propped his elbow on the table, while rubbing the other hand across his forehead. "Well, since I brought it up, I guess I at least owe you an explanation. I was driving Jasmine...my wife...and Kaydie back from a doctor's appointment."

He hesitated, watching her closely as she carefully set the clothes down on the table. "At that exact moment, the Fort Worth police were chasing a bank robbery suspect on the same interstate highway. I never noticed the lights or heard the sirens, but suddenly a speeding pickup swerved into our lane from behind.

"I turned the wheel the minute I caught sight of the truck in the right-hand mirror but it was too little and too late. The truck rammed directly into our passenger door with enough force to lift the van off the ground and push it across the median and into the oncoming lanes."

Bella was struck by the pain in his voice and the pictures of terror that his words had conjured in her mind. "I'm so sorry. But this was certainly no fault of yours."

He shook his head. "I'm a professional driver, for God's sake. I should've heard the sirens. If I'd had just a few seconds' warning, I could've taken some evasive action that might have saved lives."

She could hear and see his torment as he berated himself for failing to do the impossible. "How many were hurt in this incident?"

Cal hung his head. "My...wife...and the driver of the suspect's truck were killed instantly. An innocent motorist coming toward us from the other direction and I ended up in the hospital," he told her. "It could have been much worse, I suppose."

"And Kaydie? What happened to your daughter?"

"She wasn't injured at all." He looked over to the baby's sleeping form and blinked once. "I had insisted on keeping her behind me in the car and in a specially made cocoon-type infant seat. Jasmine used to complain about how much time it took to strap her in before we could go anywhere. And she was always griping about how she couldn't reach Kaydie if she started crying."

"So your actions did save your child's life. I think you should commend yourself for being careful rather than chiding yourself for your misfortune."

Cal jerked up from the table and limped to the side of his daughter's crib. "You don't understand."

Yes, Bella believed there was something more behind his guilt that she didn't understand. Something more he'd left unsaid. But she wasn't going to push him for answers that he obviously didn't want to give. Maybe he couldn't even admit them to himself.

She stood, moving closer to his side. "Why do you race cars, Cal?" Perhaps if she changed the subject he could put his troubles aside for a while.

He glanced at her, and she saw the clouds of hurt and self-hate slowly disappear as they lifted from his eyes. "It's an adrenaline addiction, I guess," he said with a shrug.

"Hmm. It sounds a little superficial to me. Sort of a rich man's game. Is that all you want from life?"

"I don't think of it as a game, and I don't believe it's about the money or the fans…although both are nice benefits. Racers like living on the edge, taking

risks and feeling alive. I guess that description fits me
to a T.''

She glanced down at the sleeping baby's face and
saw peace—exactly the opposite from what the father's
words had described. Then she gazed at Cal, who had
turned to look at his daughter. She was happy to see
the love for his child radiating across his face, making
him seem more appealing than ever.

As he'd spoken of his racing profession, he'd certainly given off high-voltage and combustible animal
magnetism. Now as he looked at Kaydie, she found
that his charm had finally managed to turn her insides
into melted ice cream. His loving response to his child
was breaking down her defenses.

Bella surprised herself by also noticing the warm
electric currents arcing from his bare skin and zinging
through her flesh, straight to her spine. She'd believed
she'd stopped feeling these kinds of lustful things many
years ago.

But she had to admit that she was definitely noticing
them with this man. All her carefully constructed walls
seemed about to crumble around her. Was it possible
that she did still shelter a hope deep in her heart that
someone somewhere would love her one day? Or was
this simply an urgent erotic need, unlike any she'd ever
known before?

''Maybe that description fits me, as well,'' she told
him as she ordered her body back under her control.
''I take my own kind of risks to do my job on the
border.'' She didn't mention that taking risks was no
big deal for someone like her who had no family and
no love to care whether she stayed safe or not.

But the real risk would be in letting this charming
man get too close. Whatever her body felt just couldn't

matter. He was dangerous to her equilibrium and too big a risk for her peace of mind.

All the talk about risks reminded Cal of the life he'd had before any of this happened. Before the baby, and before he and Jasmine had to get married. He'd liked things the way they were back then.

Speed was what his life had been all about. He wasn't cut out to hang around a ranch wiping a kid's bottom.

As if to bring home his current miserable situation, when he twisted to move away from the crib, a spear of pain jolted through his leg straight to his hip. "Damn it." He had to stop and breathe just to keep upright.

"What is it, Cal? Are you in pain?"

"I'm fine," he retorted fiercely, as he fisted his hands and refused to bend to the pain.

She'd made a move to assist him, but when he shouted at her, she stepped back. The look on her face showed she felt stung and hesitant, exactly the opposite of what he'd been hoping to see there since the first time he'd opened his door to her.

"Damn it," he muttered again. How could he be so stupid as to push her away when what he really wanted was to get closer to her? He wanted her to feel the beginnings of need for him—not pity.

Cal stopped moving and took another deep, cleansing breath. "Sorry," he mumbled. "I didn't mean to yell. It's just that the pain surprises me sometimes. Right when I begin to think I'm healing and that I can start doing more, I do something thoughtless and have to rethink my plans."

He leaned hard on his crutch and shook his head. "God, why is this so hard?"

"Have you been receiving physical therapy for your injuries?" she asked warily.

Her voice had become so tentative that Cal immediately shrugged off the pain and concentrated his attention on Bella. "I was…while in the rehabilitation hospital. But I chose to leave and come back home." He forced a purely phony but easy smile, trying to put her more at ease. "Those doctors were all so pessimistic that I had to get away from there. I know what I'm capable of better than any supposed medical specialist who just looks at X rays."

The tension lines at the corners of her eyes relaxed as she apparently started to trust him not to bite her head off again. "I know a little about physical therapy, it was one of the things I specialized in at nursing school. What did the doctors tell you?"

"Well, they informed me that I might never walk again." He tapped his thigh and raised his eyebrows at her. "Guess they were wrong about that one."

Cal shifted his weight so he could face Bella squarely. "They're wrong about the rest of it, too. I'll show them."

"What did they say?"

"They told me I might never be able to drive a car again and that racing would definitely be out of the question for the rest of my life." He tilted his head and winked at her. "But that's just bull dung. I'll be back in a car by next season."

Bella had listened carefully to the sentiment beneath his words. He was scared. His life had revolved around racing, and now it might be lost to him forever. Her heart went out to him.

Both a recent widower and a man who'd been forced out of his life's work, Cal needed help right now. Bella decided to make sure that he had that help before she made her way back across the border. She could never leave them stranded.

Bella changed her clothes, then she and Cal talked softly about nothing important. Racing, weather, what Cal wanted to accomplish with his career. Finally she rose from the table once again to check on Kaydie. The baby was still sleeping soundly and her skin was cool to the touch.

Bella looked out the kitchen window and was shocked to find the purple and rose rays of the breaking dawn showering the yard with early-morning shadows. She and Cal had talked on longer than she'd imagined. But he was so easy to be with, so charming and enthusiastic about his work and his life on the racing circuit that the time had whizzed by.

"Is Kaydie okay?" he murmured softly.

"She seems fine." Bella stuck her hand under the baby's bottom and found it a bit wet. "She just needs changing."

As Bella started to pull off the baby's diaper, the phone on the kitchen wall began to ring. Cal stood and limped to answer it.

She didn't want to eavesdrop, but the small kitchen did not afford any privacy. Cal, at first surprised by the early phone call, soon seemed irritated with the caller.

"Listen, Cinco, I don't need your help yet," he said into the receiver. "I'll call when I want you to…"

Cal pulled the instrument from his ear and stared at it. "Son of a gun. The bastard hung up on me."

He slammed the phone down and turned to Bella. "That was my brother. He was a little hot that I hadn't called him when the baby's nanny took off yesterday.

Seems his wife has been keeping an eye on us from above.''

Bella began to ask the obvious question to that remark, but Cal quickly explained. ''My sister-in-law, Meredith, is in charge of Gentry Ranch's range pilots and air fleet. One of her jobs is to oversee the hands checking the fence lines every morning, along with watching for problems with the stock.''

''Oh?'' Bella broke in. ''Do you think she might've spotted the *coyotes* while she was checking the ranch? I don't know where they'd be in the daylight hours.''

Cal shrugged. ''I don't know. We'll have to ask Cinco. But I guess Meredith has been watching out for Kaydie and me. She flew over yesterday and noticed that the Suburban was gone but that there was smoke coming from the chimney.''

He grimaced and continued. ''On this morning's rounds she saw that the truck was still gone and began to worry.'' Cal sighed and shook his head. ''I imagine we'll be getting a visit from my brother very soon.''

''Oh, but that is good…no?'' Bella was relieved to think that someone would come to help Cal and Kaydie; the two of them seemed so vulnerable. Eventually she would have to leave, and perhaps the sooner the better—before she grew too attached to the child—and to the father.

''No,'' he grumbled dejectedly. ''Cinco's been heckling me to move into the main ranch house with him and Meredith. Our family's housekeeper is there to help with the baby, and my brother thinks I'd be safer under his roof.''

''It sounds like your brother loves you and wants what is best for you. Wouldn't that be better than trying to make it alone?'' she probed.

Cal shook his head sadly. "I know my brother loves me and he's been missing me all these years since I've been on the circuit. But he's a security freak."

Bella wondered again what he was trying to tell her.

Cal waved his hand in the air. "Cinco thinks he can save everyone and everything that happens to be within his reach. I'm sure he'd hire nurses for *both* Kaydie and me. I can't take being fussed over twenty-four hours a day."

Cal straightened and limped to the chair. "It would be the worst thing that could happen for me, and probably for Kaydie too. I need my independence to keep moving. I have to relearn how to take care of myself." He sat down gingerly and leaned on his elbow. "I can't take the chance of letting Cinco smother me with kindness. I know I must live through the pain so I can get back to doing what I love. In order to drive again, I have to be tough on myself."

Bella had listened to everything he'd said, and tried to listen to the things he'd left unsaid. "Have you thought of letting your brother and sister-in-law take Kaydie into their home temporarily? Maybe you could do better if you had less to worry about."

Cal's face turned ashen, and he stared at her as if she'd just suggested that he throw his child to the wolves. "My daughter is my responsibility. My father taught all his children to honor their responsibilities and to do their duty to their families. I just need a little help with her right now, that's all."

Bella felt as if he'd struck her. She thought she knew him well enough by now to know that he was an honorable man. She hadn't meant to accuse him of anything. And she couldn't figure out why his reaction had been so intense.

"Cal, I didn't mean that you should give up your daughter permanently. I just thought…"

"It's okay." His demeanor quickly changed and he shook off her apology. "Actually, I'd already thought of that solution myself. But I don't think Cinco will accept leaving me here alone. And…and…I think he might need more time to get to know Kaydie better."

Bella thought that last remark was a strange thing for Cal to say. Somehow his words had not made any sense to her. Even listening between the lines with her soul, the way she'd learned to do with the migrants, had not been enough to decipher his meaning this time.

But one thing had come through quite clearly. He needed help and was probably trying to find a way to ask her to stay and take care of his child while he worked on healing himself. It was something she would certainly have to consider.

An hour later Cal stood at the kitchen sink alone, washing out the few dishes they'd used for breakfast. After she'd fed Kaydie and before she'd gone to take another shower, Bella had fixed a delicious meal consisting of scrambled eggs with chopped corn tortillas and sausage mixed right in.

He'd found he enjoyed learning about the complex and gorgeous Bella. She was a better cook by far than Jasmine ever could've been. In fact, her food was as good as the Gentry Ranch's longtime housekeeper, Lupe, who made the wonderful Tex-Mex cuisine Cal had loved since childhood.

Man, he sure hoped he could convince Bella to stay on for a while. Life would be exceedingly easier—and maybe, if he played his cards right, a lot more challenging.

A quick rap on the cabin's front door caught Cal's attention. But before he could dry his hands and limp to answer it, Cinco strode through the door and into the room.

"Well, I see you're still standing." Cal's older brother gestured toward the dishes drying on the counter. "And that you can at least manage to feed yourself. Is your daughter still alive, too?"

Damn, but Cinco could sure annoy the hell out of him in less than sixty seconds. "Listen, *bubba*," he retorted, with as much emphasis on the hated baby-talk word for brother as he could manage. "We're doing just fine. Kaydie is asleep in the next room. You didn't need to break into your day just to come check on us."

Cinco ignored his remark. "Why didn't you call when Mrs. Garcia left so suddenly?" he demanded. "We've tried all along to make you understand we want you and the baby to come stay with us. Without the nanny, Meredith and I can't stand the thought of you and Kaydie trapped out here with no help and no way of escape in case of emergencies."

Cinco's expression turned softer and his eyes began to plead his case. "Things would be so much easier for you at home. We could handle everything for you."

Four

Cal threw the dish towel on the counter and turned to confront his brother. "That's just the point. I don't want your kind of 'easier.'" He shook his head as Cinco sat down, dwarfing the little kitchen table with his bulk. "I need rehabilitation…not protection. I have to learn to take care of myself before I can ever hope to go back to work."

"Cal…brother. Before you left the rehabilitation hospital I spoke with your doctors." It was Cinco's turn to sadly shake his head. "You've done an amazing job of getting back on your feet but…sometimes life throws rocks at us instead of roses. You have to learn to dodge instead of hanging tough in the middle of the road."

"You sound just like Nana Gentry used to with her 'garden philosophies,'" Cal muttered. "And it seems to me you gave me this same speech twelve years ago.

It was the wrong speech for me then and it's the wrong thing now."

"Sit down a second, Cal," Cinco softly suggested.

Cal decided it wouldn't hurt to give his leg a rest. He propped the crutch in the corner and sat beside his brother. But he really didn't care to hear Cinco's pessimistic words as he tried to make the case for Cal to come back to the main house. Cal sighed and resigned himself to the inevitable.

"Almost thirteen years ago," Cinco began. "We were all so devastated and so young that it was hard to put our feelings into the right words. Each of the three of us took Mom and Dad's disappearance in a different way. I gave up my dreams and came home to pull in my horns. I was determined not to lose anyone else from the family."

Cinco rolled his eyes at his own foolishness. "That wasn't a particularly mature or practical way to go, as it turns out." He tried to muffle a groan. "And poor, lost little Abby simply stopped developing into an adult. She became the original western version of Peter Pan, forever a tomboy with no need to dwell on her pain."

"And me, big brother? How do you, in all your new-found wisdom, see me?" Cal interrupted.

Cinco narrowed his eyes at him. "I do have a new wisdom. One born in love. I see all of us a lot clearer now that Meredith has taught me how to look."

Cal shifted uncomfortably in his chair. He wasn't sure he was ready for any more lectures from his big brother. In fact, he'd never really been ready for them.

Regardless of what Cal wanted, Cinco seemed determined to make his points. "You ran, Cal. Where I dug in and got ready to fight off the world, and when

Abby stuck her head in the ground, you took off and never looked back. You refused to admit anything bad ever happened in this life. You thought if you just drove fast enough, had enough meaningless affairs and never put down any roots, nothing really bad could stick to you again.''

What his brother was saying had occurred to Cal many times over the years. He wasn't exactly blind to what he had made of his life. But he liked it just that way.

"So what," Cal countered. "What's wrong with living life in the fast lane? At that speed you don't have time to sit around feeling sorry for yourself.'' He narrowed his own eyes at his brother. "Or…to meddle in other people's lives without being invited.''

Cinco fisted a hand on the table, but Cal noticed him pointedly relaxing his shoulders. "Life in the fast lane can get you killed, bro. And what's worse, it can hurt the people around you, too.''

Cal fisted his own hands but bit down on the inside of his cheek so he wouldn't say the things that he knew he would regret. He refused to get into it with his brother on just his second day back at the ranch. Besides, although they didn't know it yet, he had a plan for Cinco and his wife to keep Kaydie while he returned to the racing circuit. It was most important that they take the time to learn to love the baby. And Cal needed to stay on Cinco's good side until then.

"Quit running,'' Cinco pleaded. "Now's a good time. You can't walk or drive, and your baby daughter needs a dad more than ever. Let your family help you help her…and yourself.''

"Ah…hem…'' The throat-clearing noise came from the doorway, and both men turned to the sound.

Bella stood in the doorway to the kitchen, patting her face and damp hair with a towel. Cal had been so wrapped up with trying to stay quiet while Cinco lectured him that he'd almost forgotten she was still in the cabin. He wondered how much she'd heard.

Now dressed in the gray sweatpants and navy T-shirt he'd lent her, she'd tied her still-wet hair into a long ponytail that reached below the middle of her back. The clothes swam on her, of course, but she'd belted the sweats and rolled them up to keep from tripping.

Cal's attention returned to the hair…. The sight of all that black, sensual satin as she dried the ends and fluffed it through her fingers was enough to make him squirm.

Cinco jumped to his feet, nearly sending his chair to the floor. Although he'd been startled, it apparently didn't take him long to decide that Bella posed no threat. Cal watched his brother's muscles relax as he lifted his hat in greeting.

"Well, howdy, ma'am," Cinco nearly purred.

Cal began the long process of making his legs push him to a standing position. "Bella Fernandez meet my brother, Theodore Aloysius Gentry, the Fifth… Cinco…to most of us."

"Señor Gentry," she said softly as she walked toward Cinco. "I am very happy to meet the brother of my host."

Cal was stunned at how sexy she looked, even with no makeup, and clothes that swam on her. The picture she made, standing there smiling quietly at Cinco with her hand extended in greeting, was both erotic and feminine—despite the circumstances.

Cal had to pull himself together and drag his eyes away from her pure beauty in order to give his brother an explanation. "Bella showed up on our doorstep yesterday afternoon." He paused and watched Cinco's expression. "Just when Kaydie and I needed her most, by the way. I should say she saved Kaydie's life. And you need to hear how she came to be on Gentry Ranch, too."

Cinco was such an open book. Easy to read. The expressions of first surprise and then wariness flashed across his face as he shook Bella's hand and stepped back to study her.

"I think I need to hear the whole story, Señorita Fernandez." Cinco motioned for her to have a seat and then crossed his arms over his chest to wait until she sat down at the table.

"Please call me Bella. And I will be happy to tell you what I can. But first I must check on the baby." She opened the door to the baby's bedroom and slipped inside.

"Whoa, little brother," Cinco whispered after she'd disappeared. "Who is she really? And how did she get way out here? I didn't see any cars in the yard."

"I think I'll let Bella tell you her own story," Cal replied. "It's almost unbelievable. But you need to hear the whole thing. You'll get answers to some of your questions. And I bet you'll also think of a bunch of questions you didn't even know you had."

Cinco nodded. "Put on some coffee, then. I'll go round up another chair so the three of us can gab awhile."

By the time Bella returned to the kitchen, a new pot of coffee had been made and poured, and the two men were sitting with their knees touching under the tiny kitchen table. They'd found another chair and it waited for her, squeezed in next to theirs.

"I guess Kaydie's okay?" Cal asked, then didn't wait for her reply. "Have a seat, Bella."

Cinco gingerly pushed his chair back into the small space, stood and motioned for her to take the empty chair. "Yes, please sit down and tell me how you arrived at my brother's door, little lady."

She scooted around them both and slid into the waiting seat. Nearly the entire kitchen was taken up by their presence. She'd thought Cal had an imposing figure, tall and lean. But his brother, who was just as tall seemed twice as broad. Between the two of them, she felt dwarfed and barely able to breathe.

Bella mentally shook herself out of the claustrophobic impulses by remembering that she knew Cal well enough now to trust him with her physical safety. He would not let anything bad happen here. These men were the good guys, after all.

She spent the better part of the next hour telling Cinco the story of how she came to the cabin. He listened quietly and only stopped her to ask a question when he realized she'd gotten out of the *coyotes* truck on Gentry property. She told him the same thing she'd told his brother, that she had no idea of how they'd arrived at that place.

Cinco sat quietly staring down into his coffee mug for a few seconds after she'd finished. He finally glanced up, first at Cal, then turned his gaze to her.

"I suspect you're in considerably more trouble than you realize, ma'am," Cinco softly told her. "If the INS gets any inkling that you're here illegally, they'll deport you faster than you can turn around."

"Oh, but that is not trouble. I wish to return home. I was trying to find my way back when I stumbled in here."

She'd said the words quickly and without thought, but after a second she realized it wasn't completely the truth. She flicked a peek at Cal, whose expression looked as if he'd been hit in the gut. The truth was she'd really rather stay right here and help the baby—and the man who'd befriended her in her time of need.

"Yes, well," Cinco began. "Even if that's true, I'm afraid that as soon as you step across the border, the *coyotes* will find you and kill you. You are the one person who wouldn't hesitate to identify them to the Mexican authorities. You not only witnessed the illegal smuggling of human beings, you saw them commit a murder."

"I…" Bella was speechless.

Cinco's words brought the fear back to the forefront of her mind. She'd been worried about the *coyotes* finding her ever since she'd escaped from their truck. Cinco was right. They wouldn't stop looking for her on either side of the border. She'd been lulled into feeling safe here in the cabin, but she had to remind herself she wasn't truly safe anywhere.

With no real friends in Mexico to turn to, there would be no one there to offer protection. Bella knew her homeland was rife with corruption. Mexico has many good-intentioned people as well as the few bad ones, but she had no way of knowing which was which and whom to trust.

She couldn't go back. She wouldn't last one day. The fear froze her tongue. Was she doomed?

"She's staying with us," Cal suddenly announced. "The INS can just go jump in the Rio Grande. Bella's on Gentry Ranch land now and under our protection." He slammed a fist down on the small table. "Fix it for her, bubba. I've just hired her to be Kaydie's nanny. She's not leaving.''

Cal had been so panicked by Cinco's words that he'd blurted out the first thing that came to mind. In the silence that followed his loud demands, he snuck a peek at the faces of the other two people sitting at the table.

Cinco's expression could only be called bemused. Apparently not annoyed by his brother's words, Cinco seemed to be studying Cal with a new and rather curious gaze.

On the other hand, Bella's face held a myriad of expressions—none of them particularly friendly.

She was the first to break the silent aftermath, though she still seemed at a loss for words. "I..." Bella squirmed in her seat, but her eyes shot fiery arrows in his direction.

Finally she straightened and addressed Cinco. "Yes. That is right, *señor*. I wish to stay on the Gentry Ranch and be Kaydie's caretaker.''

Cinco turned his inquisitive perusal on her. "You're sure about this, Bella? I'll contact our attorney. I imagine Ray'll be able to think of some way to get the INS off your back for a while. But..." He turned a very pointed stare toward Cal. "You're positive you want to care for Kaydie...my brother hasn't coerced you into this?''

Bella shook her head and folded her arms across her chest. "I'm positive.''

"Well, in that case, you should be safe enough here with Cal. We'll find out how the *coyotes* got past the fences, but they won't get another chance. Meredith and the crew will keep a sharp lookout from above.'' Cinco rose from the table and inched his way across the small expanse of kitchen toward the door. "Meanwhile, I'll see what I can do with Ray."

He stopped at the doorway and turned back. "By the way, do you drive?"

She looked a little surprised. "Automobiles? Why, yes, certainly."

Cinco nodded. "Good. I'll have the Suburban that Kaydie's first nanny abandoned at the bus station delivered out here for your use." He reached for his Stetson. "Anything else you might need?"

Bella set her jaw and flicked a glance toward Cal before she answered. "Physical therapy equipment might be nice."

Cinco chuckled and flipped the hat onto his head. "Uh-huh. As a matter of fact, we have a whole room set up for therapy back at the main house. I'll get someone to bring a few of the most useful pieces of equipment out tomorrow."

Cal was startled out of his silence by the realization that they were discussing him. "Hey. Wait just a minute. That stuff wouldn't be for me, would it? Don't I get a say in this?"

Cinco went right on talking to Bella as if Cal wasn't even there. "I have an idea that you could make good use of a couple of laying hens, some fresh vegetables and a clothesline to dry the baby's things. Would you like me to have them delivered with the equipment?"

Bella's eyes lit up, and she nodded enthusiastically.

"And how about a horse? Do you ride?"

"Oh, yes, please. That would be wonderful," she said.

Cal was amazed and temporarily couldn't think of a thing to say. She hadn't asked for new clothes or the things he would've imagined a woman might need. In fact, it seemed to him that she'd never considered herself, asking only for practical things for him and the baby.

Cinco grinned. "You know, lady, I'm really going to like you." He tipped his hat to her and nodded to Cal. "You're in good hands, brother. See you soon." With that, Cinco backed out of the kitchen, and a second later the front door could be heard slamming behind him.

Cal used the tabletop to lever himself up on his feet. He leaned over and glared at Bella.

"Just what was that all about?" he growled. "Therapy equipment and horses? What big ideas do you have going round in that pretty head of yours?"

Bella stood and picked up the coffee cups but didn't answer his question. She wasn't exactly sure what she'd been thinking when she agreed to be Kaydie's nanny. But when Cinco had asked about the truck, pictures of transforming this cabin into a home for the baby—and her daddy—had danced right into Bella's head. If she was going to take the Gentrys' hospitality and hide out here, by heaven she would make herself useful.

"Bella?" Cal straightened and moved toward her.

With her hands full of coffee mugs, she couldn't fend off his touch. She tried to shake him by scooting around to the sink, but he used his whole body to block her way and hold her in place.

"Are you mad at me for telling Cinco you'd agreed to be Kaydie's nanny?" Cal gently laid his hand on her arm. "I guess I should've talked to you before I told him that, but…"

She shook her head and tried to ease her arm back

to her side. But her hands were still full, and she didn't want to make a big fuss. "No. It's okay. This solution seems like the best answer for everyone."

Her skin sizzled where he touched her. The two of them certainly seemed to have a special chemistry together. She looked up into the gray depths of his eyes and felt an electric tingle all the way to her toes.

Cal must've noticed it, too, because his eyes began to blaze. The heat between them flamed—and tendrils of fire licked at all her pulse points.

He leaned closer still. Her body urged her to slide right into his arms. As hot as the kitchen had become, Bella still craved the heat of Cal's body. Somehow desperately needing to experience the comfort of his strong arms, she melted into his chest and the warmth she knew she would find in his embrace.

Before she reached her goal, however, Bella caught a whiff of baby powder. She couldn't tell whether it came from Cal or if perhaps she imagined it. But either way, the clean fragrance, reminding her that he was a single dad and a recent widower, stopped her cold.

Bella backed up a small step and broke the erotic spell that had captured Cal and held him suspended in place. "Whoa." He let go of her arm and reached for the tabletop to steady himself. He'd come back to reality so fast that it had left him a little slow-witted.

"Are you all right?" She quickly placed the mugs in the sink, then spun back to help him get his bearings.

"Dang," he muttered.

"Are you in pain, Cal?"

He reached for his one crutch and straightened his back. "I'm fine. It's just that sometimes I feel like…like I've driven right out of the fast lane and landed in some bewitched place where everything goes in slow motion.''

''I'm sure that must be very disorienting.''

Pity. He could hear it in her voice. That was absolutely the last thing he wanted from Bella.

He set his jaw and scowled at her. ''Look. I don't need your help—or your sympathy.''

''Oh...I didn't mean...''

''Forget it.'' He swung his crutch, coming dangerously close to hitting Bella on the leg, and planted it a few feet in front of himself. ''All I want from you is to be my child's nanny.''

Cal couldn't stop a snarl as it replaced his usual clever grin. ''I pay caretakers extremely well. Play your cards right, sugar, and you'll go back to Mexico a very rich woman.''

Bella's face paled and she backed up a step. She looked stung. But it didn't take her long to recover.

Within a few seconds her face turned to crimson and she narrowed her eyes. She grabbed a dish towel and began wringing the life out of it.

Whew. Cal had a funny feeling she'd prefer it if that towel was his neck.

''This is the second time you've been rude,'' she finally ground out between her gritted teeth. ''There is no need to continue to insult or test me. I'm not the kind of woman that you can push into doing what you want. I'll take care of your daughter and I will assist you in your efforts to recover—because I want to help. Period.''

She slammed the towel on the counter and moved past him toward the front door. ''I'm going out for a walk.'' The front door crashed behind her with such force that the entire cabin shook on its foundations.

Kaydie's startled scream shook Cal from his second stupor of the last half hour. He went to her crib and lifted her out and into his arms.

"Yeah, I know, kid. That one was all my fault." He patted the baby on the back. "I just don't know what's wrong with me. I can usually charm my way around any woman.

"But I can't seem to help myself around either one of you." He grimaced when Kaydie burst into tears and stuck a fist in her mouth. "I don't know what you need…and she brings out the worst in me.

"What I really want is to get closer to her and have her start liking me. Instead something always makes me act like a complete idiot."

Kaydie quieted and looked up at him as if to say, "Maybe you *are* a complete idiot, Dad."

He limped them both toward the love seat in the front room. "I've never felt this way before in my life, baby girl. And I've certainly never acted like such a jerk before, either. Something inside me must be missing."

His daughter whimpered as he plopped them both down on the cushions of the love seat. "Maybe you're right." He leaned back and softly laid her across his chest. "I've got a feeling whole chunks of me have been missing for a long time, and I'm only just now noticing it."

Bella tried to slip back into the cabin without making any noise. Fresh, crisp autumn air had cleared her head. The rush of anger she'd experienced as she'd walked out of the cabin was long gone.

If she was going to help Cal recover from his wounds, the two of them would have to find a way to build a relationship that was not quite so volatile. Surprisingly, she did still want to help him.

Bella wasn't totally positive that she should help the arrogant and self-centered gringo. Except…he had certainly jumped in to help her in her time of need and she wanted to show him how grateful she was.

And then there was the love he had for his child. Every time she saw the look in his eyes as he beheld his daughter, Bella's heart did flips. No man who cared so much for his family could be all bad.

She crept into the cabin and headed toward the kitchen, determined to set things right between herself and Cal. A muffled noise coming from the direction of the small sofa caught her attention before she'd gone two steps. When she investigated, she discovered Cal was sound asleep.

He couldn't possibly be comfortable there. The sofa was tiny compared to his large frame. And he'd stretched across it so that his legs were still on the floor and his head leaned back against the far edge.

Bella moved toward him, thinking she'd gently shake him awake just long enough to move him into his own bed. But when she neared the little sofa, she realized that a second person was asleep there, as well.

Kaydie was curled up on her father's chest. His big, wide hand splayed out across her back while she rested peacefully on her tummy. Even as they both slept, Cal held his child securely in his protective grip.

The sight of the father and child was so compelling—so heart-wrenching—that it stopped her where she stood.

Oh, what she would've given to have felt that same kind of love from the man who had been her own father. But that dashing *caballero,* who had stopped the hearts of thousands of young señoritas and made even the most elderly women swoon by simply glancing their way, never paid a moment's attention to his own daughter.

Bella felt a tingle on her cheek. She reached up and found wetness there. It had been a long time since she'd had any tears to shed about self-centered concerns. There was so much real pain and sorrow in this world that crying over never having been loved seemed childish and absurd.

Her eyes blurred, and she sat down on the edge of the sofa, trying to regain her composure.

Cal stirred when a small distant sob dragged him out of his slumber. Was Kaydie all right?

He slowly came to and sat upright, cradling the baby to his chest as he rose. His child still snored softly and never moved a muscle as he rearranged her on his lap.

Well, if it wasn't Kaydie whose crying had disturbed his nap, then who…?

Cal sensed Bella's presence before he actually saw her in the lengthening shadows of afternoon. It was a bit disorienting to realize that the strong and erotic woman he'd come to both lust after and respect was sitting all alone in the dark, weeping.

"What's the matter, sweetheart?" he whispered. "Is there something I can do to help?"

"No, no," she choked. "It's just that you and Kaydie made such a wonderful picture lying there. I…thought of my own father."

Cal wondered why thinking of her father would cause her to cry. He was rather afraid to ask, concerned that her father might be dead. Since his own parents' disappearance, he'd been sensitive to other people's relationships with their families.

"Uh. You want to tell me about it? Do you miss him very much?"

She gave him a weak smile. "I have nothing to miss."

"What does that mean? Has your father passed away?"

"I have no idea where my father is. He might be dead for all I know," she answered harshly. "He wrote me out of his life years ago when I went to nursing school."

Cal brushed away a tear that was threatening to drop off her chin. "Talk to me, honey. Tell me what's hurting you."

Bella swiped at her nose and set her shoulders. "My father was a rich man's only son. He dabbled in politics, tried his hand at movie acting and taught college students when the mood struck him." She hesitated a second in order to take a much-needed extra breath. "Mostly my father and mother were members of an international jet-setter group that did as little useful work as possible.

"I'm not at all sure why they bothered to give birth to a child. I suppose I was a mistake." But that mistake had desperately wanted her parents' love, she remembered. "I worked so hard to be good...to do the right things...to make good grades in school. I wanted them to pay attention."

Cal laid a hand on her shoulder. "You could've gone the other way—been very bad in order to get noticed."

She almost chuckled through her sniffling at that remark. "There were some months when I never even caught a glimpse of either one of them. I knew my father valued 'nice' things. It would never have occurred to me to try being bad in an effort to make him love me.''

''How did you get along by yourself?''

Bella did smile then. ''I was well cared for by servants.'' Well cared for, yes. But she'd never really been cared *about*—not by anyone.

''I always wished my father would care about me like you care for Kaydie. The sight of you two curled up there together reminded me of that.''

She thought of the few times she had seen her father up close, remembering him as the most beautiful, the most charismatic human being who had ever lived. The moment he stepped into a room the whole place came alive with energy.

Cal seemed to be made in the same mold. His mere presence shook her soul. He could've also been the same kind of thoughtless and uncaring charmer her father had been. And like her former fiancé, Enrique, had turned out to be.

But there was something more to Cal. He'd been tender with his child and obviously cared about family. He was definitely not from the same mold as the other two men she'd tried so hard to make fall in love with her.

''I care about you, darlin',''' he drawled as if he had been reading her mind.

For the whole time Bella had been speaking, Cal had been absently patting the baby's back as she'd lain cuddled close to him. He set Kaydie down gently next to him on the sofa and edged closer to Bella.

''I don't like to see you so sad,'' he murmured as he placed his arm around her shoulders.

The quick arousal was a surprise. But not unwelcome.

Her pulse jumped as he slid his hand up and down her back, mimicking the moves he'd been making with Kaydie.

But with Bella, his tender touches made crazy jolts rocket around in her stomach. And when his palm moved down to cup her bottom, the jolts headed lower, too.

No. His caresses were not at all the same with her as they had been with his daughter.

"Uh...Cal. I don't think this is the right time for..." Bella wasn't accustomed to feeling hesitant or unsure. But this was a situation that threw her off course.

She bit into her bottom lip and tried to decide what she really wanted from him. But then something sharp came into his eyes, a look that had her already-rapid pulse skipping at a faster rate.

"Hell, sweetheart, don't think." He pulled her to his chest. "Just come on over here, and we'll see what seems right to do."

Five

Cal dragged Bella into his embrace. He forgot about wanting to wait until she grew to like him. He forgot that he should've apologized for being an ass. And he forgot all about the baby sleeping on the couch next to them.

He couldn't think of anything but Bella.

Her scent of soap and clean fresh air had stirred his hunger. The burned-butter color her eyes became in this light had mesmerized him. But when her tongue glided over her bottom lip, leaving a residue of glistening wetness, nothing else seemed to matter. The fantasy of sinking his teeth into that spot and tasting the liquid fire he knew he'd find took over his conscious mind and left him a babbling, yearning idiot.

It was madness. Urgent and wanton madness.

He took possession of her mouth. Using his teeth on

that bottom lip, he scraped it into his own mouth and sucked gently.

Ah...the sweet taste of her was everything he'd dreamed it would be and more. Honey and musk—with a hint of some peppery spice that had to be Bella's alone.

She made a small sound deep in her throat, a noise that seemed exactly as primitive as the need that roared through him at the moment. The minute she aligned her body to his and opened her arms wide, he responded in kind by letting his hands roam where they would.

His fingers slid down her arms, but the thick sweatshirt she wore was not what he wanted. She edged closer to him and put her hands against his chest. That did it. One of his hands moved to the silky skin at the nape of her neck.

The other hand slid down her rib cage and closed over her breast. She quaked and groaned, arching against his palm as if she'd been desperate to have him do just that.

He savaged her mouth—while her hands clawed at his shirt. Wanting nothing so much at this moment as the feel of her ripe golden skin beneath his fingers, he reached for the edge of the fleecy shirt. With one quick move, he slid his hands underneath and found the steamy heat of her body waiting for him.

Groans of pure pleasure came from them both.

He tore his mouth away from her lips and moved down the satiny skin of her neck. "I've wanted to do this from the moment I first laid eyes on you."

She threw her chin up so he could feast on her throat. "I know," she whispered. "I've wanted..."

Cal began to drag the offending sweatshirt up and

over her head. Skin on skin. The insane madness urged him onward ever faster. She wanted him; she'd said so.

He'd have what he needed now and finally get her out of his system. They'd worry about all the rest of their problems later.

But just then Kaydie stirred beside him and made cooing baby noises in her sleep. The rest came back into his mind with a clash of softer needs.

Bella felt Cal move back from her before he physically withdrew. She opened her eyes and tried to focus on him, her vision blurred by passion and need. His pupils were still wide and black and hungrily drank her in.

But too soon he dropped his arms to his sides and the look in his eyes changed, telling her he was putting distance between them.

He cleared his throat. "Bella." He said her name as if it pained him just to be near her. "That wasn't smart."

"I know. I…" Her hands were shaking, so she folded her arms over her chest and tucked them into her armpits. "Why? Why wasn't that smart?"

Cal turned his head and reached for his child. "We haven't known each other long," he mumbled over his shoulder. "And you need to…" When he picked up the baby, Kaydie awoke and started to cry.

Bella had never been more miserable in her whole life. Even being lost by herself in the countryside had not made her feel so all alone.

Cal didn't want her. He'd probably remembered his lost wife when they'd just kissed and had decided that he wasn't ready for a new relationship.

But he was the lucky one. He had his memories *and*

he had his daughter—and more than that, he had his entire family behind him.

Bella had nothing—and no one to care about her. Feeling empty and raw, she stood.

"Where are you going? I thought we should...talk," Cal murmured as he lifted Kaydie into his arms.

"I need a moment. If you'll excuse me?"

But Kaydie had other plans. The baby screamed and reached her arms toward Bella.

Cal appeared to be frustrated for a moment, then looked up at Bella with pleading eyes. "Help? I guess she knows who's best for her."

When Bella didn't make a move, his look changed to desperate. "Please?"

Here was her reason to go on. The same reason that had always given her the will to live. It didn't matter so much that no one had ever loved her—not when she was needed.

And both of the Gentrys in this house badly needed her help.

The next morning, after Bella fed and bathed the baby, she wanted to find out more about the place where she had found refuge. But Cal had not appeared for breakfast. So far. She hadn't even heard him stirring.

Last night each of them had spent most of the evening lost in their own thoughts. They'd eaten a light supper, she'd put Kaydie down for the night and slipped into bed.

Her night had passed fitfully, with nightmares of *coyotes* and lost children forcing her awake several times. But Kaydie had slept soundly. Apparently her bout with the cold was almost over.

Bella hesitated to awaken Cal. He hadn't really agreed to having her help him with therapy yet. And after yesterday's passionate kiss, she thought it might be best to stay out of his bedroom until it became clearer that their relationship would be limited to friendship.

"Well, *niña,* let's you and I go for a little stroll, shall we?" Bella finished fastening the baby "running" shoes to Kaydie's feet and picked her up under the arms.

The baby grinned with a toothless giggle as she dangled her feet above the surface of the bed. Kaydie lifted up each foot in turn as if she readily agreed that, indeed, a walk would be a good thing.

"Sorry," she told the little girl. "You're not quite ready to actually walk yet. Especially on the uneven ground around here. But I'll think of something…"

Bella spotted her bundle in the corner. She'd washed and folded her filthy clothes yesterday, but had been more than happy to put Cal's clothes back on. His sweats were soft and warm. Her one pair of jeans and shirt had holes and stains that could never be removed.

"I think this should work." Bella picked up her old shawl. It was threadbare and hadn't added much in the way of warmth, but it would work nicely as a sling to carry the baby.

She found a woolly cap and sweater for Kaydie and arranged her against her chest like the Native women did. "There you go. Now you can see our new neighborhood, too." The baby was tied snugly against her, facing out to view the world.

Bella left Cal a note. Just in case he awoke and wondered where she'd taken his child.

Surveying the area around the cabin, the two newcomers spent about an hour scouting out their new place. They found the nearby creek and admired the willows and pecans growing at its banks. Then they saw a windbreak that someone had erected to shelter animals from the elements.

"Maybe we should keep our new horse here, baby. What do you think?" Bella murmured.

The little girl didn't answer. But when Bella checked, she found Kaydie's eyes were wide-open as she quietly took in every detail of her surroundings.

When Bella figured that the baby would be getting tired, she headed back toward the cabin. She was also curious to see if the baby's daddy had arisen and wanted his breakfast by now.

When she walked up the slight incline to where she could view the cabin, it surprised her to see people climbing in and out of several trucks. And there was lots of activity near the house, too. "Look at that, Kaydie. We have company."

As they came closer, she spotted Cinco—and Cal. Cinco was supervising men as they took pieces of equipment off a truckbed and carried them into the house. Bella recognized a set of walking bars and weights among the things they'd brought.

It was harder for her to see what Cal was doing. He'd leaned up against another truck and was talking to a beautiful, blond woman. She was tall and statuesque in pants and leather jacket.

The swift jolt of jealousy caught Bella off guard. Cal was grinning at the other woman, while the wind was playing games with his chestnut-colored hair. The sun had kissed his cheeks, deepening his skin color to a wonderful shade of bronze. He looked young—and so handsome that Bella nearly wept with the pure joy of seeing him.

She wished he would someday look at her the way he gazed at this Anglo woman. As soon as she'd had the thought, Bella recanted. No, she chided herself. He's just another ladies' man. And he will never be more than simply a patient and perhaps a friend. There was no "someday" in their future.

Things must always remain that way, she thought. Her sanity and her heart depended on it.

"Bella!" Cal called out the minute he spotted her walking toward him.

The lights in his eyes danced over her as she came closer. "Well, just look at Kaydie, sleeping peacefully in her little cocoon. What a wonderful idea."

He reached for her arm and pulled her closer. "Bella, I want you to meet my sister-in-law, Meredith."

Cal was beaming, totally in his element surrounded by women. "Meredith is the best ex-Air-Force pilot you'll ever meet…and she's a damn good sister, too."

Ah…the wife of the brother. Bella relaxed her shoulders and the corners of her mouth.

"Hi, Bella. I'm glad to meet you." Meredith took her hand but didn't smile as she studied her. "I've heard a lot about you."

"Oh? I hope what you heard was good, Señora Gentry."

"Hmm. Too good. Cinco did nothing but rave about the exotic beauty that had arrived on Gentry Ranch. I wasn't about to let him come out here again without me."

Bella was a little confused. "But why…?"

Cal chuckled. "Cinco and Meredith haven't even

been married a year yet. She was jealous and had to come check you out for herself, sugar.''

"Of me? You have no reason to be jealous of me, *señora*. You are so beautiful.''

Meredith drew her shoulders back and stood tall. Her face was flaming and she frowned at Cal. But then she turned back to Bella and smiled.

"You are every bit as pretty as Cinco said, Bella. But I wish you'd call me Meredith.'' Meredith's gaze landed on the baby and her eyes lit up as if the little one was a wonderful present she'd just been given. "I love the way you're carrying Kaydie on your chest like that. Ohhh… She is so adorable in her little cap and sweater. Do you think I could hold her a minute?''

Bella put a hand under the baby while she untied the shawl. "Certainly. She fell asleep a little while ago, but she's probably ready to wake up and visit with us.''

Meredith took Kaydie into her arms as the baby opened her eyes and looked around. Meredith held her close and jiggled her up and down, waiting until Kaydie was fully awake to play with her.

"You know, Bella,'' Meredith began as she patted the baby. "I saw a backpack baby carrier that can convert to a front pack in a store last week. It accomplishes about the same thing as your shawl…except it might be a little sturdier. Maybe you'd like to go to town with me and see if the thing would fit you and Kaydie.''

"Oh, that would be very nice. I'd like to see about getting some new clothes to wear, as well.'' Bella liked this woman, the warm smile Meredith bestowed on her and the way she fussed over the baby.

She turned to Cal, who'd been extremely quiet and

still for several minutes. "Would you be all right by yourself for a while if Kaydie and I went shopping?"

"No." The sharp word escaped his mouth before he had a chance to call it back. "I mean…I need you to drive Kaydie and me to her new doctor. We can stop at the store afterward if you wish."

Meredith eyed him suspiciously. "That's fine. Bella and I can shop another time." She changed her expression back to a sweet smile for Bella. "By the way, Cinco wanted you to supervise the men who're building the chicken pen back near the kitchen door." She pointed toward the house.

"Oh, the laying hens!" Bella looked excited. "I should go…"

"Go ahead, sugar," he told her. "After you do that, you'd better go check on the herd of horses my brother had delivered a little while ago, too."

"Herd?"

"Hell, yes. I consider three mares a damn herd."

"I should go, then." She reached a hand to touch Kaydie's head. "The baby will be okay?"

"She'll be fine," Meredith told her.

Bella pulled her hand back, nodded to Meredith and marched away toward the men who were struggling with the chicken wire. Her long fine hair jauntily swung above her swaying hips.

The minute she was out of earshot, Meredith rounded on him. "Just which one of us was jealous, brother?"

"Isn't she spectacular, Meri? Those big brown eyes and that expressive mouth…"

"I guess you've got it bad, if you don't even want to let her out of your sight long enough to take a shopping trip." Meredith planted a soft kiss on Kaydie's forehead. "She's only been here a few days, Cal. Don't you think you should go a little slower? She's a foreigner in a strange place with no friends. Rushing her might be a big mistake."

Cal cocked an eyebrow at her. "*We're* her friends. And I'm not rushing her." He shrugged a shoulder. "But I can't seem to help being an absolute jerk around her, either."

The irritation that sprang to life with Meredith's words went away as quickly as it came. He knew that he'd been the cause of all his own aggravation. And Cal was becoming seriously concerned that he might never be able to figure out the reasons why.

A man had to do what a man had to do. And some things just weren't manly.

He fidgeted in the passenger seat once again and swung a look back to check on Kaydie. His leg was killing him, but there was no way he'd mention it at the moment.

His daughter slept like…well…a baby in her carrier in the back seat. While Bella concentrated on the dirt road that would take them off the Gentry Ranch and onto the blacktop road leading to town.

She drove slowly and carefully. And Cal thought he might go nuts. When Mrs. Garcia had driven them out there a few days ago, he hadn't minded riding along. But somehow, when it was Bella driving, he felt weak and small. How was he ever going to be able to stand riding with her until the time came when he would drive again?

"There's no one else that uses this road, sugar," he mumbled and tugged at the confining collar of his dress shirt. "You could pick it up a notch or two."

She just smiled but didn't make a move to change her speed. "You can relax, Cal. I will get us there in one piece and on time for Kaydie's appointment with the doctor."

Relax? Now there was a concept. Just being this close to the most erotic woman he'd ever met was keeping his nerves strung tighter than a newly installed timing belt. Add to that the fact that he couldn't remember ever letting a beautiful woman drive his car with him in it before, and nothing at all added up to his being able to simply lie back.

"Does sitting this long make your knee hurt worse?" She threw him a concerned look. "I can stop for a rest if you need one."

"Just keep going." The faster she drove the sooner he could get out of this car altogether.

"Uh, Cal…" she began hesitantly. "Will Kaydie's doctor also be your family doctor? Can he look at your knee and give you something for pain if necessary?"

"I don't need anything for pain." Even if the damn thing ached like crazy sometimes. "Joe Domingo owns a general practice clinic in town, but I've never been his patient. He's only been in Gentry Wells for about fifteen years. He came here to join old Doc Stevens. But after Doc retired, Domingo hired a couple more doctors to do the work.

"I'm not positive I trust him," Cal continued. "He's a little too slick for my taste. I intend to watch him carefully while he examines Kaydie. I'm not sure what kind of a doctor he is. He seems more interested in politics. After he got the clinic going, he moved into the old Castillo Ranch next door to the Gentry and ran for the country judge's office a couple of years later. That was right at the time my parents disappeared."

She blinked a couple of times after he mentioned his parents, but quickly changed the subject. "Will you let me help you with your rehabilitation? I'm very good at physical therapy…and I'll make a great slave driver."

"Terrific," he muttered. "Another slave-driving therapist. Just what I need."

But it *was* just what he needed. And he knew it.

And what better way to be near to Bella? If she would be helping him with therapy, she'd have to touch him occasionally, wouldn't she?

"Do you think you can handle Kaydie, the chickens and horses…and me?" he probed.

"Kaydie and the chickens and horses will be easy."

They looked at each other, then both laughed out loud.

"Yeah. I know I wouldn't be a piece of cake to handle," he grinned. "But still you're willing to try?"

"Of course." Bella slowed the car as they came near the blacktop. "We will take a short break here, I think."

"Break? I told you I'm fine." He wanted to keep going.

"This is not for you. I need to change the baby and give her a little water."

"You need to change her again?"

Bella smiled that enigmatic smile once more and turned off the ignition. "*Sí.* It will not take long."

As she pulled Kaydie out of her carrier in the back and laid her across the seat to change her diaper, Bella asked, "Don't you want to step out of the truck?"

"Naw. I'm fine." He wasn't really, but he'd be damned if he'd let on. "You're good with Kaydie. I wish her mother had been half as good."

"Your wife had difficulty with the baby?"

"My wife had difficulty with everything…mostly with me." It pained him to admit it. Had never occurred to him to even say it out loud before.

Bella shot him a confused look. "You were very much in love with your wife?"

"No." He heaved a long-suffering sigh. "I never loved Jasmine. And I doubt that she ever loved me…or Kaydie."

"But then, why…?"

"Why'd we get married?" God, he'd wondered that himself so many times. "I'd known Jasmine a long time because she hung around the tracks. The groupie women like her who follow the drivers are known to everyone. And she was gorgeous…in an obvious sort of way.

"After a big win at Texas Speedway, I got a little carried away with the celebrating and she and I…well. I'm not particularly proud of it. But I insisted we get married when I found out Kaydie was on the way."

"Ah…I think many marriages begin that way, no?"

Cal had always thought so. "Maybe. But in our case the wife and mother was the one who felt trapped. She made it very clear she had no intention of settling down and becoming domesticated, as she put it.

"I had plenty of money to hire caretakers for the baby, so I thought we'd be okay anyway. I'd been careless, but I was determined to make up for it by making her happy. I figured I'd hire the nannies and all of us could travel the racing circuit together."

"But this did not work out?" Bella questioned.

He shook his head but couldn't bring himself to tell her the rest of it. Couldn't bear to put a voice to the fact that he'd been the faithful one and his wife had been the one to cheat.

Maybe he shouldn't have told Bella about his loveless marriage. Meredith might've been right. Was he pushing this new relationship too hard?

But Bella had been so open, so easy to talk to.

Ha! Easy relationships with women seemed to be his specialty. Perhaps he should rethink this one.

Cal thought about Jasmine and both of the times he'd been careless with her. He'd already made a huge mess of several lives. He swore never to go down that road again.

Care and time, he reminded himself. He still wanted Bella. Hurt from the want, in fact. But he would be careful with her. Never again would he be casual about an affair.

As it turned out, Dr. Domingo wasn't in his office when they arrived. He'd been called away to an emergency meeting of the County Commission. Cal convinced Bella that they could do their shopping, and when one of the other doctors in the clinic was free, the receptionist would call them on the cell phone.

Within an hour they'd bought the pack that Meredith mentioned. Cal removed his khaki blazer and red tie, slung the pack over his shoulders and had Kaydie snuggled safely inside before Bella could laugh at the idea of the tall, masculine man carrying a papoose.

He dragged Bella by the elbow through the store toward the women's clothing department. "Come on," he urged. "Let's see what they have, at least."

"I'd rather not, please. I don't have any U.S. money right now and I need to—"

"My treat," he said, beaming.

Bella tried to dig in her heels but found herself sliding along the slick flooring instead. "I do not need your charity. I will earn my own money and pay my own way."

Ignoring her, Cal came to an abrupt halt directly in front of a mannequin of a women dressed in a long gauzy skirt with a white peasant blouse casually draped off her shoulders. The skirt was multicolored in shades of sage green and deep purple. It was feminine and yet looked practical, as well.

Bella coveted the sensual outfit the moment she looked up and saw it. But still...

"There. Now that looks just like something you should wear. Why don't you try it on?"

She shook her head, but the words to deny herself wouldn't come.

Cal took her by the shoulders, turned her to face him. "You won't take money from me to be Kaydie's nanny. And you won't take new clothes from me..." He scowled and raised an eyebrow. "Even though I would be giving them to you as a gift with no strings attached.

"How about we make a deal?" His face lit up in a wide grin. "I'll hire you to become my physical therapist. I promise I'll do whatever you tell me to do with no complaints. But you have to promise to take a salary for doing it. Deal?"

"Well..." She couldn't think of anything wrong in the proposal, but it still seemed a little like charity.

"Great! Now go try that on and I'll look for some work clothes for you. Will jeans and flannel shirts be okay?"

Six

"We don't have to do anything special," Cal insisted as they walked through the kitchen door later. "Meredith and Abby will bring more food than you can imagine. And Cinco promised he'd bring the ice and beer."

Cal had sprung the family "poker" night on her when they'd only just arrived at the cabin from the doctor's visit. "I have to check on the chickens and the horses," Bella fumed. "How can we have visitors when I haven't even had a chance to settle the baby down yet?"

The man was annoying the devil out of her. She'd only arrived at this cabin three days ago and she barely knew her way around. How could she help him entertain when she hadn't even had a chance to clean house?

"No sweat, sugar," he said with a breezy grin. "They aren't visitors. They're Kaydie's and my family and they won't care a bit whether she's settled down. They'll probably rile her back up when they get here anyhow.''

He was so attractive and charming when he wanted to be. The sight of those gray eyes alive with energy and pleading his case caused a jolt down her spine.

She thought back to their shopping trip and his joy at buying clothes for her and Kaydie. He'd looked so handsome in his white shirt, tie and coat. But when he'd bought the baby a little pink jumpsuit that had yellow ducks and rabbits on the bib, Bella thought her heart would crack.

The yearning to be someone that he truly cared about nearly doubled her over with want. But she knew better than to wish for impossible things, and she was sure Cal would always be a womanizer just like her father. So she pushed the need out of her mind and buried it deep inside.

"If you'll put Kaydie down in her crib for a nap, I'll feed the horses and check the chickens," she suggested as she handed the baby over to his waiting arms. "I'll be back in a few minutes to clean the house. I'm anxious to meet the rest of your family. And I suppose this poker game tonight will be as good a time as any."

"Sure. Okay," he said with little enthusiasm. "I'll manage with Kaydie if you promise to have some fun tonight."

Later, with the poker game underway, the kitchen and the front room of the cabin were lit up and the sound of laughter and family could be heard clear across the range. Bella had happily greeted Cinco and Meredith, who'd flown all of them there in a helicopter for the evening's game.

But to Bella's great surprise, Cal's sister, Abby,

turned out to be a rather petite but sturdy ball of energy. The young woman's hands were calloused from hard work, and her nose was freckled with the obvious signs of being outdoors. Bella liked her instantly.

She was slightly less easy around Abby's new husband, Gray Wolf Parker. A dark and imposing Native American, Cal's brother-in-law was solemn as he scrutinized her.

But Gray warmly took her hand when they were introduced. And later she noticed how he gazed at his new wife with an all-consuming look of love in his eyes. A little jealous stab pulsed through Bella but she quickly banished it, the same way she'd shoved aside the need for Cal earlier.

How could she not like Gray or anyone else who loved with such great passion? As a matter of fact, she liked all of Cal's family.

"Ray…he's our family attorney, tells me the INS has agreed you can stay in the country temporarily," Cinco told her privately when he came into the kitchen for another beer. "They weren't thrilled about you staying on the Gentry, but now they're looking at this as a good place for short-term asylum."

He grinned at her. "We sort of…convinced them it was the right thing to do." Cinco opened the longneck beer bottle and took a swig. "Meanwhile, the sheriff and the Border Patrol are working together, trying to find those *coyotes*…and figure out how they knew enough to travel across Gentry Ranch property."

"Did you find where they came through your fences, *señor?*"

He took the bottle from his lips and tilted his head. "It's Cinco, remember? And no, the fences on this side of the ranch were still all in one piece." He looked thoughtful a moment then smiled again. "I'm surely grateful for that, too. Meredith would've had a fit if it turned out she'd missed a downed fence when she was on her rounds."

He took another swig and swallowed. "And if she's unhappy—I'm absolutely miserable." He chuckled and then focused on Bella. "Don't worry. We'll be patrolling that section of fence at night. If the *coyotes* are going through there and repairing it themselves, we'll find them."

Bella saw the look of deep love in Cinco's eyes when he talked about his wife. Once again a tiny prick of jealousy stabbed at her heart.

She drew a long breath but didn't say anything.

"By the way, sugar," Cinco began. "I've been meaning to tell you how glad I am that you stumbled in here. The family has been real concerned about Cal and the baby…mostly about Cal, I guess. Your coming here has already changed him…made things easier. Hell. We're just happy to have you here."

"My being here has changed Cal?" she asked. "I don't understand. How?"

He shrugged a shoulder. "I shouldn't have said anything." Cinco's expression seemed sincere. "Cal hasn't been much for family ever since our parents disappeared. And then after Jasmine's death he walled himself up in solitude. In the hospital he didn't want to see us. And it was a good month before he even asked about the baby."

He shook his head and continued. "I suppose when life beats you up long enough, you stop letting anything get close." Cinco took one last swig from the longneck. "We were amazed when he decided to come home to the ranch to heal. But instead of wanting to be with the family, he installed himself out here in this cabin that Abby and Gray had just fixed up, and refused all of our efforts to help.''

Slightly surprised by some of his words, Bella thought back to what she'd overheard on her first morning. Cinco had said something about Cal running away from life because he couldn't face his parents' death. Perhaps a few things made more sense now.

Cal loved his family and Kaydie, Bella was positive about that. But there were still so many questions.

''Now that you're here, my brother's a little looser somehow,'' Cinco told her. ''For instance, he let us bring all that equipment and other stuff out here. And this poker game…. Well, he never would've agreed to something like this if it weren't for you.''

Bella simply smiled at Cinco, then mumbled her excuses, saying she needed to check on the baby. Cinco so clearly cared about his brother. She was jealous of that family tie, too, but at the same time she was glad Cal had someone to love him like that.

She knew now that Cal was injured in ways that weren't so obvious when she'd first met him. And more than ever, Bella was determined to find a way to heal him before she had to leave the country.

Cal banged his good shin on the edge of a chair and cursed the darkness. Something, some noise or quiet disturbance of air, had awakened him at this early-morning hour, so he'd come to check on Bella and Kaydie. And he vowed no damn out-of-place chair would keep him from it.

It might've helped if he'd turned on the lights. But that hadn't seemed like the prudent thing to do at the time. If something was wrong—if the *coyotes* had discovered Bella and were just outside the door—well, Cal didn't want to alarm anyone unnecessarily.

The poker game had been over for hours. As much as Cal had loved to be around his family again, he'd been grateful when the last goodbyes were said. He couldn't have stood another sympathetic glance from any of them. He loved them, to be sure. But he just didn't want to deal with the raging emotions his entire family had brought with them.

He was having enough trouble figuring out what he wanted when it came to Bella. He'd tried desperately to tell himself it was just lust. That after that mind-blowing kiss they'd shared, all he wanted from her was her body.

It wasn't the truth, of course, but lust was something he could manage. On the other hand, trying to sort through his ''feelings'' was a downright impossible task. Just look at what a bad job of it he was doing when it came to Kaydie.

The moon suddenly peeked around a passing cloud. Moonlight flooded the front room of the cabin and Cal finally got his bearings.

He hesitated in the doorway from the kitchen, surprised to see Bella sitting on the sofa feeding Kaydie in the dark. What a tender sight they made together.

His baby seemed sleepy and contented as she drank from her bottle. Bella looked like a perfect mother as she whispered softly and rocked Kaydie in her arms.

For some reason the vision made him feel lonely. His own mother had whispered to him in that exact same way, he remembered, and a yawning chasm of memories threatened to envelope him in the dark. He shook them off and set his jaw.

He needed to get his equilibrium back. Bella put him

off balance. There had been no memories, no loneliness, no yearning before Bella came. She'd stirred up something inside him, and he wanted his peace back.

Cal figured once they gave in to their attraction, that would be the end of it and he could get back to the way things had been. And it couldn't be too soon to suit him.

"Ouch!" The damn corner of the wall reached up and slammed him in the bad knee, causing the exclamation to escape from his lips before he could stop it.

"Cal?" Bella looked up and tilted her head. "What are you doing up?"

"I heard something," he huffed. "Thought you might be in trouble and need help."

"We're fine." She glanced down at Kaydie then drew her gaze back up to meet his. "Your daughter was hungry earlier than usual. I don't like making a baby wait to eat. They don't understand the concept of timetables."

"Oh. Well…" he mumbled. They didn't seem to need him at the moment. He grabbed the corner of the wall, prepared to turn around and head back to bed.

"Wait," she called out to him. "Uh. Since you're up, maybe you could sit for a while and keep me company until Kaydie finishes her breakfast."

Yeah. He could probably do that. After all, he was wide-awake now.

He limped toward the chair next to the sofa. "If you really need someone to keep you company, I guess I can manage to help you out." Cal thought he heard Bella make a small disgruntled noise in her throat at that remark, but it was probably just Kaydie burping.

Once he'd settled his body into the overstuffed chair, he decided to get Bella talking about herself. He figured that was one good way to put her at ease. And he needed her to like him… It was suddenly important that they become friends. He wasn't going to make the same mistake with her that he'd made with his wife.

"So…" he began. "Are you happy with life in general, Bella?"

She glanced up at him. "I suppose. I haven't thought about it."

"I don't care for mine at the moment," he interjected.

"Is it your profession…the driving…you miss?" Bella guessed.

Cal shrugged, but wasn't sure she caught the movement in the dark shadows that engulfed them. "Mostly," he admitted. "Driving didn't ever feel like a job, though. It was always more of a game."

"A dangerous game, I think."

"The danger never seemed to bother me…before."

"And now?" she probed.

Cal answered with the first thing that popped into his head. "Now I think too much." Dang. He wondered how they'd ended up on this subject.

He heard her shift the baby in her arms, but the moonlight had disappeared and the room had fallen into darkness once again.

"Thinking too much might not be a good thing on the race track, yes?" Her voice was clear, soft and concerned. "I mean, that might make you hesitate. And maybe it could get you killed."

Thinking too much might just be the death of him, for sure. But it wouldn't be while driving.

"It's late, sugar." He was about to take the coward's way out and knew he was starting to make stupid remarks. "I mean it's early. And my knee hurts. I think

I'll go back to bed for a while. We can finish this discussion at another time.''

Bella tried to hide her irritation with Cal as he twisted in his saddle, and she stemmed the urge to go to his aide. ''Cal, please stop grumbling,'' she muttered with as much cheerfulness in her voice as she could manage—considering the circumstances.

It had taken all her strength just to prepare, arrange and start out on this outing she'd planned. Having to soothe Cal's injured feelings at this point qualified as a little more than she could handle.

''Tell me again why you're so damn sure a ride and a picnic will be good for me.'' He'd turned around in his saddle to speak to her and she saw he was still steady on his mount. But obviously he was having some pain.

She'd expected that. However, it hurt her to see the lines of it cross his brow. Over the past week she'd come to like this irritating man. A physical therapist should not be too sympathetic when it came to making a patient squarely face his pain, though.

To make injured muscles relearn their proper uses, a patient must work through that pain. Think past it. Push it aside and go on, even when that was the last thing he wanted to do.

Cal had been trying so hard to do whatever she'd asked—until today.

''Just keep your horse moving, please.'' She aimed the comment toward his back as his mare moved in front of hers.

When he was feeling good, the man could charm the flame right out of a fire. But when he was in pain, he was absolutely the most annoying...

Kaydie shifted in her carrier on Bella's back and Bella had to remember her riding posture. She'd been competent on horseback since she was a little girl at boarding school. It had been one of the things that "mannered" girls had had to learn. But she'd found that she loved riding. Most especially, she'd decided she liked it here—on the open Texas plain.

"There's the river and the trees you've been looking for," Cal shouted over his shoulder. "Can I get off this damn mare now?"

"Please wait until I dismount and can assist you," she grumbled as she pulled her own mare and the pack horse up under the pecan trees. "Remember how we organized it when you got on the mare's back at the cabin? And remember how I said I would aid your dismount when we arrived at the river?"

Cal grumbled under his breath but stayed in the saddle while she and Kaydie slid off the back of her mare. Bella knew it must be difficult for a man who'd been riding all his life to suddenly have to be assisted on and off his horse.

She was impressed by how well he was doing, even though his pride was taking a beating. After just a week, Cal had regained much of the strength in his upper body. That was good news and bad. Like most patients, he tended to want to use that strength to do all the work for his painful lower limbs.

Bella insisted on this ride in order to force him to use his legs where he could not depend on his muscular arms to help him along. But those arms of his had been a great help when it came time to mount the mare. He'd practically dragged himself onto the mare's back with pure strength of will. That, and a little help from Bella

and the mounting box that Abby brought over from the
main ranch.

"All right," Bella said after she tied down all three
horses. "I'll get the box to help you."

"No way," Cal sputtered. "Just come over here so
I can lean on you when my bad leg hits the ground."

With a long-suffering sigh, Bella did as he asked.
"You do not have a bad leg," she told him for the
thousandth time. "Your right knee and hip have been
replaced with joints made out of space-age materials.
That does not make your leg bad. It is good. And you
will be able to walk on it again soon." *If* you'll do the
things I ask of you—even though they will be difficult
and embarrassing, she urged silently.

Once Cal was back on solid earth he straightened
and pretended that nothing was wrong with him at all.
He helped Bella pull Kaydie and the carrier from her
back. Then he spread the blankets and tarps in the
shade of the trees.

After they were settled and fed, Bella coaxed the
baby into taking a nap. It was a warm autumn day and
the sky above the leaves on the trees radiated a clear
crystal blue. A few flying insects buzzed nearby, but
they seemed more interested in the bright-orange wildflowers growing in crazy profusion all the way from
the riverbank to within arm's reach.

Cal leaned back against some packs at the base of a
tall pecan tree. His eyes were half-closed and he finally
looked at peace. Bella leaned back, propped on her
elbows, and studied him at her leisure.

He was such a wondrous sight since the pain had
disappeared from around his eyes and now that his
mouth had taken on an easy tilt at the corners. She

thought she could happily lie here and look at him all day.

This past week, as they'd been working with weights or when she'd been massaging his sore muscles, she'd tried hard not to look at him as a woman looks at a man. He'd been a patient, nothing more.

But now. Now she could see the bulges under his shirt that she'd help make. The lightweight, long-sleeved shirt strained to cover the muscles across his chest. He'd left the top couple of buttons open, and a few of his chest hairs curled daringly with the freedom they'd found there.

Little twinges fluttered in the vicinity of her belly. The spasms felt almost like hummingbird wings beating wildly against the inside of her body.

Long before Cal opened his eyelids and found her staring at him, the heat of Bella's eyes on his body burned into his gut. "You doing all right, sugar?" he drawled.

"Hmm. Yes, I am full and fat and lazy." The words came easily from her mouth—slow and sensuous and sweet.

She lithely stretched like a cat. A sleek, black-haired panther, Cal thought. Instinctively his hand moved to caress her smooth golden skin. But she rolled just out of his reach.

He drew a long breath and got more than he'd bargained for. Sure, the smell of early fall was in the air. The weeds on the plain had dried like hay and the cedars were ready to sap. But the scent of Bella teased him unmercifully with tangy aromas of raspberry soap mixed together with the sugary smell of the chocolate cake they'd had for dessert.

Damn, but it had been a long week.

He'd known the physical therapy would be difficult—and painful. He remembered what it was like from the rehabilitation hospital. But what he hadn't known was how hard it would be to have Bella's hands constantly on his body and not be able to do anything about it. And he meant that word *hard* literally.

Cal had spent the past seven days in a constant state of arousal. He'd tried to concentrate on other things. Like the last ten years of Formula One racing statistics. Or mentally going through the entire manual of the stock-car association's rules and regulations. Nothing had worked.

If he couldn't manage to charm his way into becoming her lover soon, he wasn't sure his poor body would stand the strain of fighting both the pain of therapy— and the pain of wanting her.

Using his forearms, he leaned over and inched his body closer to where she lay. "You look good enough to eat, Señorita Fernandez," he murmured in his most charming tone of voice.

She opened her eyes wide, then immediately narrowed them when she saw how close he was. "If you wish to move around, I will help you stand. It would be somewhat difficult with the uneven ground here, but we could…"

Anger flashed, then quickly subsided. "I thought today was my day off. You said we wouldn't work if I'd come on this picnic."

It intrigued him no end that his charm still seemed to be lost on her. He knew there was heat between them. The kiss they'd shared had been an excellent example of that. And sometimes he would catch her staring at his body.

He'd done everything he could think of to make her

trust him and like him. He knew she'd already taken to Kaydie. The signs of her love for the baby were written all over her. It wasn't that Bella wasn't capable of love, then. In fact, he suspected she was ripe with potential in that regard.

So what was wrong with him? Cal decided to push her a little and find out.

"Have you ever been married?" he asked, then realized that might be too out of the blue. "Or engaged maybe?"

"What a very strange thing to ask all of a sudden," she said dryly.

But she rolled over and leaned up on one elbow to talk to him. "Yes, I was engaged once. Luckily, we never married."

"Did you love him?" he inquired bluntly.

Bella hesitated a moment. The look in her eyes spoke of great sorrow. Cal had never seen that particular look there before and it bothered him.

"Yes. I thought I was madly in love with Enrique. He was an intern in the hospital where I studied nursing." Her eyes took on a dreamy look as she thought of her past. "What a dashing figure he made in his white coat, too. All the nursing students were fascinated by him."

"What happened between you?"

She raised an eyebrow. "What happened? If you mean did we have sex, that's none of your business."

"On, no..." he stumbled, chagrined at the foolish way he'd asked the question. "I don't mean the intimate details. I just meant why didn't you two ever marry?"

She relaxed her shoulders, and her lips softened into a wry smile. "Enrique was like a prince in a fairy tale.

When he told me the stories of how he would be helping our countrymen by bringing health care to the migrants traveling toward the United States, I was...charmed. He was sexy and intelligent and I thought marriage to him would be like a dream come true.''

''So he's the reason you work for the church on the border.'' Suddenly a dark thought occurred to him and he had to blurt out the question. ''He wasn't the man who was killed was he?''

She shook her head and wrinkled her nose. ''His stories propelled me into doing the church's work. But to Enrique they were just good stories to tell the ladies. After his internship, he decided there was a lot of money to be made in private practice. He took a residency in dermatology and...he married a woman doctor who owned a big clinic in Houston.''

She sat up and shrugged her shoulders. ''I was so devastated I wished I could just curl up and die. I'd been so sure he truly loved me. It was...very foolish of me.''

''Oh, Bella. I'm sorry.'' Cal's first reaction was anger at the bastard who would tell stories and pretend to be in love just to win a roll in the hay.

In the next moment the memory of doing some of those same sorts of things himself came back to haunt him. But he'd never left anyone devastated and wanting to be dead. He was sure he hadn't.

''Some men can't be trusted,'' he finally said. His voice sounded hoarse and reedy.

''I thought all men were that way. But now I wonder. Your brother and brother-in-law are trustworthy. Are they not?''

''Yes, I suppose that's true.'' He thought of his family, of the superior examples of manhood he'd so casually ignored. "And my father was the most admirable man who ever lived. You could trust him with your life. If he said he'd do something, the world coming to an end wouldn't stop him from getting it done."

Having said that, the image of his dad telling him he would back his efforts on the racetrack with all the power of Gentry Ranch came to his mind. The very next week his father was gone forever. He hadn't kept his promises.

"And you, Cal," Bella put in. "When you knew a woman was carrying your child, you insisted on marriage, even though there was no love. That was trustworthy. I'm sure your father would've been proud of you."

Cal wondered what the old man would've had to say about his plans to abandon his only daughter and run back to the carefree lifestyle of the racing circuit—even though Kaydie would be in much more capable and trustworthy hands with Cinco and Meredith than she would be with him. He rubbed the heel of his hand against his chest and tried to block the ache by turning his thoughts back to the beautiful woman beside him.

"Just doing one thing right doesn't make me a person to be trusted. I managed to kill my wife off, remember?"

Bella rolled on her back and gazed up through the leaves, wondering what she should say to that. The soft blue skies had given way to steel-gray clouds. Surprised, she discovered that in the quiet, she could hear the rumble of thunder in the distance.

The man beside her had many things going on inside him. He definitely felt guilty about his wife's death. More so than the circumstances seemed to call for.

But there was more than that there, too. Cal's whole demeanor had changed when he'd mentioned his father. It seemed odd that his loss had not healed over the years. But since she'd never known the love of a parent, she had no way of guessing how such a loss might affect a son.

She chastised herself for trying to psychoanalyze the man and closed her eyes for a moment. When she opened them again, Cal was staring at her in a way that was hard to ignore.

His eyes smoldered with desire. That much was easy to read. But as she gazed into the stormy, darkened depths she discovered more than hunger. For the moment his eyes carried sorrow and a pathetic little-lost-boy look that caused her heart to twitch.

He reached over and plucked up one of the brightly colored wildflowers. Rolling it absently between his fingers, Cal studied it for a second then bent to slide it behind her ear.

Touched, Bella sat up and placed a kiss on his cheek. She'd meant it as a thank-you. As a silent prayer for him to find his way. And as a helpless apology for his suffering.

For a second he remained perfectly still, but the heat radiating from him grabbed at her soul and set fire to her body.

He lightly touched her cheek, ran a knuckle along her jawline. The touch was too tender. Too gentle.

Right now Bella needed the flame of him, not the sweetness. She latched her hands on to his shoulders and firmly placed her lips against his.

Without a second's hesitation, Cal crushed his mouth down on hers and deepened the kiss.

Seven

Nothing in her life had prepared Bella for this. This raw, ragged need twisting in her belly.

How could she have known there would be this much desire between two people? Enrique's kisses were warm and inviting, but they'd never combusted inside her the same way as the conflagration Cal had started.

Her head reeled with a flash of heat. Automatically she lifted her hands to Cal's neck, drove her fingers through his hair. He groaned and ran his kisses down over her jawline to the tender skin at the base of her neck.

Plastered against his chest, she still couldn't get close enough. Her hands went wild, tugging at his hair, digging into his skin, pulling him ever nearer.

He quickly moved back to her waiting lips. His mouth was clever, hot and richly male. His tongue tan-

gled wildly with hers, demanding attention. Sucking at
her lips and tongue, the sensation he kindled drove a
blaze deep within her body. Down between her thighs
the bonfire caused at first heat—then wetness.

Cal heard the tiny moans deep inside Bella as he
closed his mouth over the tip of her breast right through
the flannel shirt. He wanted more of those moans of
pleasure. She was so wild. Such an energetic lover.

He felt her trembling as he moved over to cover the
other breast with his mouth. The erotic jolts sent need
shooting directly to his loins.

Pulling her body closer, he pinned her wrists and
lifted them above her head to have better access. Bella
groaned as her head fell backward and she arched her
body against him.

More. He had to fill himself up with her, and her
with him. Now. Right now.

But…right then, a roll of far-off thunder ripped
through his brain, just as the first few drops of freezing
water hit the back of his neck. The rain, splashing
against the heat of his roaring desire, effectively smoth-
ered the fire.

Oh, the smoke of it still smoldered, to be sure. And
the hardness of his body was slow to respond to the
change. But his brain had awakened from its sensual
fog, and he knew he must pull away from the tempting
sizzle that was Bella.

He lifted his head and gently put her arms back to
her sides. Not quite able to let go just yet, he rubbed
his hands up and down her arms, willing her to open
her eyes.

She did, drowsily lifting her lids to look at him
with some confusion. "What—" she cleared her throat
"—what is the matter?"

A few more splashes of cold rain managed to fall through the leaves above their heads. "It's raining, honey. I think maybe we'd better..."

Kaydie's sudden cries changed the atmosphere around them in an instant. Bella pulled away from his hands and stood to check on the baby.

"Oh, do not be distraught, *niña,*" she cooed. "It's only the rain."

But Bella quickly lifted Kaydie from her carrier and covered her head with a baby blanket. "We should be heading back to the cabin now, I think," she told Cal.

Cal made the torturously slow effort at standing. "Yes, that would be best." His head agreed, but his body still argued the point.

Bella handed over his daughter and then made short work of cleaning up their picnic area. Cal helped her with the baby carrier, and before he knew it they were ready to go.

It grated on him that she had to assist him into the saddle. But he gritted his teeth and surprised himself when mounting the horse turned out to be much easier this time.

The pack horse was ready, the grounds spotless and all that was left to do was for Bella, along with the baby on her back, to mount the mare. Cal turned his horse in a circle and realized that the rain now came down with driving force.

"Honey, you'd better pull the tarps back out of the saddle packs so we can have cover on the way home," he warned.

She turned to do as he asked. But as she dragged the first heavy, green cloth from the pack horse's back, a lightning strike cracked the plain about a quarter of a mile from where they stood. The ground shook, a brilliant flash of white light illuminated the world and a startling shot of thunder fractured the air around them for miles.

Kaydie shrieked and Bella's body jerked in reaction. Worse, all three horses spooked, folded back their ears and jerkily danced sideways in protest.

Cal had his mare under control in a moment with one firm word and a couple of well placed hands and thighs. But Bella was overwhelmed, what with her hands and back full and two extremely scared animals to settle.

He reached down and took the tarp from her. Then he urged his mount over toward the pack mare. When he was close enough, he used his hands and his voice to soothe the frightened horse. Meanwhile Bella did her best to calm down both her mare and Kaydie.

His efforts paid off with the pack mare. But just as Bella had quieted the baby and was about to climb into her horse's saddle, the ground shook and another crashing boom of thunder rattled through the air.

"I can't keep the mare from bolting," Bella screamed over the clamor. "I can't take a chance with the baby."

Without giving it a second thought, Cal reacted. "Give me your horse's reins. I'll tie her behind my mare." When he'd accomplished that, he directed Bella to tie off the pack horse directly beside the other mare.

Still skittish, Bella's mare rolled her eyes back. There was no way Bella and the baby could mount her. "Give me your arm," he demanded of Bella.

"What? Why?"

He could see the first real sense of panic growing in Bella's eyes. Lowering his voice and speaking with as much control and patience as he could manage, Cal tried to soothe her the same as he'd done with the mares.

"You and Kaydie will ride in front of me. It'll take a little longer for us to ride back that way, but the baby will be safer and we'll all stay drier."

She stood there, shaking her head, the indecision written across her features. Lordy mercy, but she was one gorgeous woman.

"Bella, listen to me." He hesitated until he had her full attention. "The lightning has moved on. All that's left is a heavy rain, but the mares are still skittish. Keeping us together on one mare is the only answer. I'll take care of you and Kaydie. Trust me."

"But your bad knee…" she stammered.

"My knee isn't bad," he said with a forced grin. "You said so yourself. Now trust me to know what I'm doing. Give me your arm and I'll help you up."

The sleeting sheets of rain had turned to icy prickles of mist by the time Cal maneuvered their little party over the first section of ranch toward home. Settling Bella and the baby in front of him had been easier than he'd thought it would be.

Guiding his mare in a slow but steady gait, Cal chuckled at the idea of what a sight their little party must make. He'd draped the three of them completely with the extralarge tarp. Meanwhile, the other two mares drooped along behind them, splashing rainwater and mud as they went.

Kaydie had snuggled down into her dark warm cocoon between him and Bella and was soon sound asleep. Since then, there had been nothing but crackling silence to stir the air.

Every once in a while, though, he'd torture himself by taking a whiff of Bella's hair. Or he'd drive an electric current through both of them by shifting the reins in his hands and folding his arms around Bella's inviting body.

As they rode on, it occurred to him that now everything had changed. No longer was it the most important thing in the world for him to talk Bella into his bed. Although that prospect still held a lot of promise and certainly most of his interest.

But she'd trusted him enough to hand over her life into his hands. He couldn't begin to imagine when anyone else had ever deliberately taken such a drastic step with him. And that meant something. Something so profound it might take him weeks of thinking to figure it out.

Bella leaned back on her heels and grinned at Kaydie. ''What a big girl you are,'' she praised.

Kaydie was sitting upright without the aid of pillows for the first time in her life. And all it had taken was a small bribe of a cracker, which the baby had now proceeded to stuff partially into her mouth. Of course, the little one ended up with more chubby fist in her mouth than cracker.

In the three weeks since their picnic was rained out, Bella had grown to love this child with everything she had. She knew it was foolish and that her heart would break when she had to leave, but there was no curing it.

It seemed there would be no stopping her foolish heart from falling in love with the baby's daddy, either. The man was rash, annoying and beautifully tender. She lay awake at night just yearning for him to touch her once more.

Bella shook her head at such nonsense. He hadn't

made a move in her direction since the day they'd ridden home in the rain.

However, he'd been working hard at learning to walk without a crutch. She'd let him lean on her when he was too tired to go on alone, helped him unlace his orthopedic shoes late at night and massaged his sore muscles when they'd cramped with unbearable pain.

She'd had to touch most of his body. But still only as a nurse. And he'd never once made a move to change the direction of that relationship, either.

Bella tried to tell herself she should've expected him to lose interest. That's what happened with womanizers, wasn't it? But nothing she did or said could change the fact that she wanted him to want her. It wasn't smart, but it was the way she felt.

The kitchen door swung open, and Cinco strode through into the cheery room. "Howdy, family," he drawled. "Where's the daddy of the house today?" He flipped his hat onto a hook.

"Well, howdy to you, too, Uncle Cinco," Bella said, mimicking his accent. "Cal is soaking in that bathtub you so kindly had installed."

Cinco and Meredith both spent several days a week bringing things out to the cabin, playing with the baby and helping Bella with the animals or the housework. Cal's sister, Abby, hadn't come quite so often because, in addition to their regular work, she and Gray were remodeling the ranch house Gray had inherited from his stepfather when he'd died. But the newlyweds came as often as they could.

"Dang. Something sure smells good." Cinco took a deep breath and grinned. "Whatcha cooking, little sister?"

She knew the endearing nickname did not mean the

same thing to Cinco that it did to her. But it gave her a warm tingle in her soul every time he used it.

Bella stood and picked Kaydie up off the floor, dropping cracker crumbs behind her. "Those are the beans. Today is the day to cook the pinto beans." She dusted off Kaydie and checked her diaper. "I'll be making chicken and rice later, if you want to stick around for supper."

"Chicken? You're not going to cook one of the laying hens are you?"

She laughed. "Of course not. I'm not sure I could actually ring a chicken's neck…even if I wasn't friends with it in the first place." Bella put Kaydie in her high chair. "Fortunately for me…Lucy, Gracie and most especially Mabel…Meredith brought several fryers and a couple of whole chickens when she stocked the freezer last week." She turned to get the baby another cracker.

"Hold on a second. Why 'especially' Mabel?"

"Well, she hasn't been laying like the others, for one thing." Bella threw her hands on her hips. "She nips at me when I go to collect the eggs, for another. And yesterday she tried to organize a breakout."

Cinco laughed until tears came into his eyes. But before he could speak, she heard Cal moving around in the bathroom.

Bella checked Kaydie and started to excuse herself to go help Cal put on shoes. When she turned, Cinco picked Kaydie back up out of her high chair and plopped her on his lap.

Then he waylaid Bella with a look and a raised hand. "Wait, sugar," he urged. "I have something important to tell you."

"But I have to go help…"

At that moment Cal appeared in the doorway, wearing jeans but no shirt or shoes. "What's happened, brother?" he grumbled. "You figure out how your fences were breached?"

Bella hissed out a breath at the sight of Cal. Every time he stepped into view, she had to fight a reckless urge to fling herself into his arms. But when he appeared like this, his skin and hair still glistening from the bath, his muscles bunched and firm from working out, she had to blink her eyes twice in order to keep still.

"Have a seat, Cal," Cinco mumbled. "You'd better hear this, too."

Cal settled himself at the table.

Cinco watched him closely. "Hey. You made that trip without your crutch. You're steadier than I've seen you since the accident." He reached over and punched Cal in the arm. "Way to go, bro. You'll be dancing again soon."

Cal scowled. Bella noticed he'd done a lot of that lately. For a man whose grin had probably broken enough hearts to fill a grandstand, he hadn't cracked so much as a smile in days. She'd thought all along that he must be in pain, but today she wondered if it might be something else.

Cinco ignored his brother's mood and turned his attention back to Bella. "I took several calls today about you. The news isn't good, sugar."

After handing Kaydie a spoon to play with, Cinco continued. "Ray has been in constant touch with the authorities. Seems he has several old friends in the FBI, and they're telling him that your case is about to become an international incident."

"My case? What is my case?" Bella was stumped,

and a sudden chill caused goose bumps on the back of her neck.

Cinco smiled at her, but his eyes remained serious. "The Border Patrol and the Texas Rangers have been working with the authorities in Mexico trying to locate those *coyotes* you saw commit murder. The State Department had to get involved when the Mexican authorities wanted to know why you were not sent back to help identify them."

"But…if they have not found them yet, how could I—"

"Right," Cal chimed in. "That's totally phony… like maybe someone on the Mexican side wants to get their hands on Bella…to shut her up."

Cinco nodded. "That's exactly what the FBI thought. They're calling her a material witness to a federal crime of alien smuggling and insisting that she stay in the U.S. until the *coyotes* can be brought to trial."

Bella was stunned. How could she have become embroiled in the middle of what seemed like two countries squabbling?

"Ray and a couple of agents will be coming out to talk to you tomorrow," Cinco told her, then turned to Cal. "Our esteemed county judge, Dr. Domingo, has also been calling wanting to talk to Bella. He apparently has a brother who is the aide to the governor of the state of Coahuila."

"He would be a very important man," Bella advised.

"What the hell does Joe Domingo have to do with Bella?" Cal exploded. "I don't know why, but I've never trusted the guy. This sudden interest by a big-shot brother is all bull. I don't want him anywhere near her."

Cinco gave one quick shake of his head and lifted Kaydie to his shoulder. "Easy, brother. The FBI doesn't much care for this sudden interest by such a heavy-duty bureaucrat from the across the border, either. They're investigating, but they don't want Bella to talk to anyone but them until they can get a better handle on what's really going on."

"Fine," Cal grumbled.

Restless and tied up in knots as usual, Cal stood and moved to the counter to get a glass of water. God. He was actually starting to enjoy being edgy and irrational.

His hunger for Bella had grown hot enough to boil his blood, he knew. But the constant, painful steam of it must've also fried his brain. Or else his brain must have lodged somewhere below his belt during the long hours of physical therapy.

All Cal knew for sure was that he'd decided against trying to get closer to the sexy Bella. But he sure as shooting didn't want her to be hurt in any way. Nor would he just stand aside and watch her be used as some kind of pawn in an international game.

He took a swig of water and offered some to Cinco and Bella, while considering what had made him so touchy. After their picnic a couple of weeks ago, it had occurred to him that he'd almost lost it with Bella. Another minute or two without the rain and he would've been inside her and watching the passion bubble up in those stunning brown eyes.

And when would he have thought about protection? Certainly not until it was way too late. How could he have been so stupid? You'd think having one child because you were stupid enough to unzip your pants without protection would be enough. Wouldn't you?

Cal glanced over to where Kaydie sat babbling away in baby talk to the side of Cinco's head, trying to get his attention. She was a pretty cute little kid, he had to admit. But he still planned to figure out a way to leave her with his brother—and certainly not create a new mess to have to deal with.

"So, anyway," Cinco continued. "Expect Ray and the FBI tomorrow. And I'll keep our distinguished county judge from finding out where you are." He stood and handed the baby over to Bella. "I've got to be getting back."

Cinco headed toward his hat, still on the hook by the door, but stopped midstride. "Aw, dang. Abby would've had my head if I'd left and forgot to invite y'all to her and Gray's barbecue Thursday night."

Bella looked up at him with wide eyes. "They wish for us to come to a big party?"

"What're we celebrating?" Cal asked.

Cinco chuckled at Bella. "Not a huge party by Texas standards, sugar. Gray doesn't much care for crowds." He turned back to Cal. "They've finished the remodeling of the old Skaggs place, and they want to show it off to their family and friends."

Cal nodded and glanced around the cabin. "Judging by what he did to this place, Gray does good work. I'll bet his stepfather's place turned out fantastic."

Cinco drove a hand through his hair and flipped the Stetson over it. "Well, it's not the Gentry, but I'd say it would come in second best. Better see it for yourself."

"We'll be there, bubba," Cal said, knowing full well if he didn't, Abby would pitch a fit. "We wouldn't miss it."

The damn afternoon was too nice. The sun shone a little bit too brightly in soft-blue skies to suit Cal. Crisp autumn breezes brought the smell of mesquite smoke and Texas prairie just a bit too gently to make him happy. He didn't want to feel so stuffed and lazy after a great meal.

In fact, it annoyed the hell out of him that every dad-blamed thing had to seem so perfect.

He didn't need this family barbecue to remind him of happy times growing up here. The last thing he wanted to do was remember how loved and safe and free his parents made him feel back then. That time was gone forever, and Cal intended to keep his concentration focused on returning to his current life—the track, the traveling, the parties.

The only block to that focus was the exotic and wildly erotic Bella, whose presence in his life and whose troubles with her life were causing no end of lack of concentration on his part. He glanced past the pit, where earlier a side of beef had slowly rotated on a spit, and found her talking with Meredith on the other side.

Bella looked spectacular standing there with the sun in her hair, making it look like a shiny black paint job. The honey color of her skin had turned to bronzed gold in this light.

Cal sighed, leaned on his new cane and stuffed his other hand in a back pocket. A couple of days ago, when Ray and the two agents had come for their interrogation, her eyes had grown narrow and dark with concern. Today her eyes were back to their normal chocolate color with those bright sparkles at the edges.

He didn't know why, but he didn't want to ever see that black look in her eyes again. If her eyes were going to go dark, it would be because of passion—not fear. Of course, soon he wouldn't be able to see the color of her eyes at all. Soon he would be well enough to go back to racing, and Bella would become a distant memory.

Somehow that fact just wouldn't sink into his heart.

The other fact he was having trouble with was Kaydie. Right this minute, his sister-in-law was cuddling the baby and bouncing her in her arms. Cal knew both Cinco and Meredith had come to love his child—the way he'd planned. And the timing seemed perfect to ask them about taking her into their home permanently. He would even be willing to consider letting them adopt her, if that's what they wanted.

But when he'd been talking to Cinco earlier, the words he'd needed stayed locked inside him. Now, as he tried to ignore the ache in his chest while he watched Kaydie giggle, Cal fought the nagging strains of guilt. Could he simply walk out of her life and never look back?

Across the way, Bella laughed with Meredith as she tickled the giggling baby in her arms. Bella tried to fight the jealousy at seeing the two females, looking so alike and seeming so happy. It was not her place to want to be the mother to this child. Cal would find a beautiful, blond Anglo woman to marry, and they would make a pretty picture all together.

Oh, but her heart ached at the thought of never seeing Kaydie or her father again. Of going back to the loneliness and the emptiness she'd come to realize had been her life.

She turned away from Meredith and the baby and caught a glimpse of Cal, standing by himself next to the picnic tables, watching them. Bella gulped back the lump in her throat—apparently a little too loudly.

"He's certainly a handsome man, isn't he?" Meredith said with a chuckle.

Bella could only nod, but she couldn't force her eyes away from his gaze.

"You've fallen in love with him," Meredith stated. "I figured that you would. Cal's charming, handsome, wounded. More experienced women than you have made fools of themselves over him."

Bella froze at Meredith's words. Was it true? Could she possibly be falling in love with a charmer like Cal?

She didn't want to face the fact that she was making a fool of herself with yet another man who wouldn't love her in return. Bella was aghast at her own stupidity. Of all things. It was true. She'd allowed herself to fall for the absolute worst possible person.

She swung back to face Meredith and her own foolishness. "Yes, I guess I have fallen." The time for lying to herself was over. "But he does not show the same interest. He doesn't want me. And soon I will be going back to Mexico. And..."

She'd run out of excuses not to be devastated and felt the sting of tears as they clouded her eyes.

Meredith laid a gentle hand on her arm. "He hasn't...you two haven't...?" She cleared her throat. "It's definitely not Cal's style to hold back. I wonder if—"

An elderly male voice rang out across the yard and Bella turned around to see who was calling to her. "Señorita Fernandez, I need to speak to you a moment, please.''

Ray, the Gentry family attorney who'd brought the FBI agents out to meet her yesterday, hurried over.

''I didn't see you here earlier, Señor Adler. Did you want something to eat? I'm sure that Abby would—''

''I've just arrived, Bella,'' he said. ''I don't want to eat. I've come to tell you something.'' Ray took a deep breath. ''It's more bad news, I'm afraid.''

Bella tried to steel herself, but her curiosity kept her holding her breath. What else could they want from her?

''The sheriff called,'' he began, ''to say that they'd found a locked railroad car, sitting in the sun on a long-forgotten siding. Some kids were playing there and noticed a funny smell. When they finally told their families, the parents called him to come check it out.''

Bella's skin began to crawl, but she wouldn't let it throw her off. This could not have anything to do with her.

Ray took off his hat and wiped his brow with the back of his hand. ''It took the sheriff a while to break the door down. And when he did…he found… I'm sorry, Bella, but he found twenty-eight Mexican-national men, all dead and stacked on top of one another in the sweltering car.''

''What?'' She couldn't quite hear what he'd said. A roar had started in her ears and it was making her light-headed.

''The FBI is on the way,'' Ray continued in a hoarse whisper. ''They believe these are the same men that came across the border with you. The ones that let you out of the truck. They're going to want you to look at some pictures to see if you can identify any of them.''

When the truth sank in, the stab in the vicinity of her stomach came hard and fast. It doubled her over and left her breathless—reeling. No it couldn't be true. She wouldn't let it be true.

But the sympathetic look in Ray's eyes told her what she didn't want to believe. The men that had been so kind. The ones who had saved her life. They were all gone? All?

The air left her lungs with a whoosh, and she fell to her knees. "No…no…" she cried. *"Dio, ayudame!"*

The sunlight turned to fog. And the last thing she saw was the brown Texas dirt as it came rushing toward her face.

Eight

Before he could consider what he was doing, blind instinct moved Cal to where Bella had fallen. He pushed Ray aside and knelt beside her.

She was so deathly pale, so still. "What the hell happened to her?" His hands trembled as he felt for the pulse in her neck.

"She's had a terrible shock and fainted, Cal." Meredith put a firm hand on his shoulder to reassure him as she turned and called out to Cinco.

Meredith had Kaydie in her arms and couldn't bend down to see about Bella's welfare. But Cal wanted to take care of her himself anyway.

"Fainted…sure…she's okay. It's going to be okay." He wanted to drag Bella up into his arms. To rain kisses over her face and wake her up. Instead he made himself move slowly. He brushed back the hair that had covered her face and forced air out through his lungs in order to calm down.

He picked up her hand and squeezed the icy cold fingers, willing her to be all right. Bella groaned—and relief burned through his gut. Thank God.

Cinco was suddenly behind him and dragging at his shoulders. "Cal, you can't kneel. You'll reinjure you're knee. Get up. I've got her."

Ray stepped to Cal's side and pulled him up by the arm.

"Maybe we'd better call the doctor." Cinco was rubbing Bella's arms and trying to get the circulation going.

"Absolutely not," Cal declared. "We'd end up with Dr. Domingo, and I won't have that man anywhere near her. I don't trust him." He stopped and peered down as Bella blinked open her eyes. "Is she going to be okay?"

"We'll take her into the house," Cinco told them. "Get her some water. She'll be okay." Lifting Bella up in his arms as he stood, Cinco turned around and marched off toward Abby and Gray's home.

Meanwhile, Cal turned raised fists to Ray and Meredith in a blind white-hot rage. "What the devil did you say to her?" He wanted to punch the man. Rip apart anybody or anything that stood in his way.

"Let me tell you what's happened while we follow them inside," Meredith soothed. "This wasn't Ray's fault. He had no way of knowing how his news would affect her."

After he'd heard the whole story, and after Bella had fully regained consciousness, Cal's legs stopped shaking. But his disposition was as foul as ever.

Those bastard *coyotes* had locked innocent men into

a wood and iron deathtrap with no food or water and no way out. That sort of thing unfortunately happened by accident on occasion. But this time they'd meant to kill them. Their intent was to leave no witnesses.

"Can I borrow your pickup?" Cal asked his brother when things had calmed down.

"What for? You can't drive it."

"Watch me, bubba." He headed toward the yard, determined to see if the keys were in Cinco's truck as they'd always been before. "You still carry rifles in the back of the cab, don't you?"

Cinco caught him by the shoulder, spun him around. "What's going on, Cal?"

Cal swung back to him, but deliberately left his fists at his side. "I'm taking Bella to the cabin, where she'll be safe. I figure I can drive standard with my left foot if I have to, but I'm sure I'm okay to drive. My knee is strong now. Don't try to stop me."

Cinco held up his hands in surrender. "Whoa. I'm on your side." He cocked an eyebrow at Cal and grinned. "You think you can do a better job of keeping her safe than the rest of us, you go right ahead and do what you have to do."

"Fine," Cal snapped back at him. "No one knows how to get to the cabin except the family and a few hands. I want her where no one can find her, where I can watch out for her. Where we can be…" He trailed off as he remembered his daughter. "Can you and Meredith keep Kaydie for a couple of days? Just until the feds get a better handle on where the *coyotes* might've gone."

Cinco narrowed his eyes at him but answered in a gentle tone. "Sure. She won't be any hardship. In fact,

Meredith will be thrilled to be able to dote on her full-time.''

"Great," Cal murmured with quiet determination. "I'll go tell Bella to get ready. Are the keys in the truck?"

Bella fussed and fumed about Cal driving the pickup and about leaving the baby behind. But in the end she'd been too exhausted to do anything more that merely rest her head on the back of the seat and let him do things his way.

Actually, she was torn between being pleased that he was moving around so well and scared that it would mean he would no longer need her. As soon as this trouble with the *coyotes* was over, Cal would go back to his life and she would never see him or Kaydie again.

"You sit and relax. I'm going to make you a little dinner," he told her when they entered the cabin. "Then you can take a nice hot bath and go to bed. Things will look better after a good night's sleep."

She'd started to say she would fix her own food and that things were not going to look a bit better no matter how much she slept. But he seemed so determined, she kept quiet.

He wasn't at all awkward in the kitchen like she'd supposed he would be. She sighed and guessed he was a man who naturally excelled at anything he chose to do.

Cal could do so many things with his life. Good things. Things for the betterment of mankind. Bella wished she could make him see that. But she knew it was not to be. He was still set on going back to the racing circuit, and her time with him grew shorter with every breath she took.

And that was the thought she kept with her as she ate the stew he'd fixed and then took her bath. The man must care a little about her to show such concern—mustn't he?

There had been passion in his eyes when he looked at her before.

She wanted to feel his arms around her one more time before he left. One more kiss. Would that be so bad?

Bella decided to go to him tonight. To thank him. To be close to him. She knew it was a little like flirting with fire, but the relationship was almost over anyway.

Just one kiss. Certainly, he might laugh at her. But the risk seemed slight. And the reward could be so great.

She stood in front of Cal's small shaving mirror in the bathroom and played with her hair. Compared to Meredith's shiny gold braid, Bella thought, her drab black strings were pretty sad. She brushed it. Then she pulled it back with a piece of yarn. Then she tore out the yarn and brushed it over her shoulders again.

There was nothing she could do about the pathetic state of her face, either. She didn't own any makeup, had never had much use for the stuff. But a little lipstick might've been a nice touch. Ah, well.

She brushed her teeth—twice. Then, sneaking out of the bathroom and into Cal's room to look for something to wear, Bella cursed herself for not having bought the frilly robe Cal had wanted her to have. She'd thought at the time that good solid cotton panties and a bra would be more useful, and besides, she loved wearing Cal's sweats to bed. When she did, it seemed like a part of him was there, too.

But just now, she wanted something a little more, uh, sexy. Bella went to Cal's closet and found what she'd sought. His fancy white dress shirt. The cloth was so fine and smooth.

She slipped off the sweatshirt she'd thrown on after her bath and slid her arms through his long sleeves. Oh, the shirt felt so satiny against her bare skin. And the hem hit her thighs exactly where she'd imagined it might. Covering the important parts, but only just barely.

Bella rubbed her cheek against the soft material at the shoulder, smelling Cal's aftershave. Then she quickly buttoned up the shirt. She stood for a minute considering. Unbuttoning all but one button, she raced out of Cal's room before she lost her nerve.

Bella went looking for Cal in the dark. None of the lights were on in the cabin, but illumination from tonight's full moon streamed through the windows and gave her enough of a glow to see clearly.

She found him standing at the kitchen window, staring out into the darkness. He was wearing his jeans with no shirt or shoes again.

That sight knocked the breath right out of her lungs. Bella lost her nerve and turned to go. But in the dark she hit the open door. "Oww," she gasped.

Cal turned. "Bella? Are you all right? I thought you'd gone to bed."

"No. I'm not sleepy. I wanted...I wanted to thank you for everything you've done." She took two steps in his direction then hesitated. "I'm sorry to disturb you. I'll just leave you alone."

He was beside her before she could make another

move. "No, wait." Cal only had to touch her arm and she leaned into him.

His body heat enveloped her, warming her soul. She took a deep breath and put her arms around his shoulders to give him a grateful hug. But the moment she touched his bare skin she knew that she'd made a mistake. She'd gotten too close.

She felt the muscles across his back jump and bunch. His movements made her nipples hard.

Cal must've felt her, too, because he pulled back from the embrace and stared down at her chest. Even in the shadows of the night and with his eyes lowered to her breasts, Bella could see the hunger written all over his face.

He did want her. She'd known it all along.

"What the hell have you got on?" he growled.

"It's just one of your shirts. Do you mind?"

She watched as he forced his gaze back up to her face, and saw him grimace. But he didn't answer her question.

He fidgeted a second, but didn't move away from her. "You need to button up. It's chilly in here."

He reached to do up the first button for her, but when his knuckles skimmed her bare skin under the shirt, he froze. "Go to bed. Please," he groaned. "I can't think straight when you're this close."

The words stopped her for a second. But he'd nearly choked getting them out, and they'd sounded thick, raspy. She decided to stay anyway. Just one kiss. That was all she wanted.

"Bella…" The look on his face was indecipherable, but his eyes had turned to steely gray. "Please leave. I've been standing here in the dark watching the plain because I can feel those *coyotes* out there…somewhere. I'm afraid I've made a mistake bringing you here."

She peered around him to look at the black night through the glass of the kitchen window. "Have you seen something? Heard something?"

Cal reached up and gently took hold of her shoulders. "No. But I don't need to do that to know they're out there." He squeezed her shoulders, as if to push her away. But the push never came. Instead his fingers massaged…caressed.

He forced his gaze over her shoulder and refused to look into that gorgeous face. "Go to bed." Furious with himself and aroused beyond belief, Cal tried to retreat.

But his feet and hands stayed where they were. Too close. Too intimate.

Bella stood her ground. "I have to thank you." She splayed her hands across his chest and lightly kissed his chin.

Cal's blood was raging. This was wrong. She was so special. So giving.

But his brain was muddled with desire. He couldn't think clearly and the roar of the blood pulsating in his veins blocked his good intentions.

Staggered with the passion he saw in her eyes, Cal leaned against the kitchen counter to keep himself steady. It was too much. She was too much. She was everything.

Before he could stop himself, he swooped down and captured her mouth. The taste of her was wild and hot, with a faint touch of peppermint toothpaste. He stopped breathing and tried once more to back away.

"Take me," she whispered in his ear. "I know you want me. Take me now."

Every shred of his control snapped. Every sane thought disappeared with the torrent of flaming need.

He gripped her hair, yanking it back to expose her neck. She let out a little gasp, but her eyes darkened dangerously and her breath quickened.

"I want you, Bella—give me everything." Now he would finally have what he'd been needing for so long—the whole world of Bella.

"Yes…yes," she whimpered, with a tremble.

He vowed to taste every inch. To light her body with burning desire then cool her down—only to reignite the flame over and over. Cal dove in, planting his teeth in the soft, vulnerable curve of her throat.

Her body jerked against his, and she groaned with the shocking pleasure of his desire. She'd pushed him into a wild, savage passion, and it made her lose her mind. She craved more of the tingling pain and erotic gratification. More of his mouth and teeth on her.

Then she was floating, felt the room spinning. She lost her breath as he lowered her to the tiny bed in Kaydie's room. Bella lifted her arms to drag him down with her.

But instead he reached over to her chest, grabbed a handful of his shirt and ripped it open. The button snapped off and exposed her fully to his view. Bella folded her arms over her chest automatically.

"Oh, Bella…you are so beautiful," he gasped.

Cal stood there, looming over her until the shock of her nakedness gave way to the demands of his body. He pushed aside her arms and lowered himself beside her.

"You're all that I imagined and more. I've been starving for you…."

Running his finger down her chest, from the base of

her neck to her navel, he licked his lips. "Hungry for this…" He replaced his finger with his mouth and tongue, licking and nibbling as he went.

"And famished for this…" He covered one nipple with his mouth while he pinched and rolled the other between his fingers.

Bella's body jumped, and she had to dig her nails into the blanket to keep her from lifting straight up into the air. Gasping, she found she couldn't breathe. It was too much. Every muscle, every fiber inside, even every bone surged with her.

"Wait! I can't…"

But his mouth was ravaging her tender flesh with tongue and teeth. Laving…nipping…sucking so that she felt the pull all the way down between her legs.

She fought for air. Fought to touch him, the way he was touching her. Running her hands over his arms, shoulders and chest, she reached for his waistband and zipper. But his hands were on her body first, exploring tender creases, tickling shivering responses from unknown places. And sending her spinning past reason. Past control.

Bella went wild under his hands. She writhed, bucked, reached…begged. Cal craved more. He craved the curves of her. The burning sensation of her skin under his mouth.

He'd lavished her navel, tasted the sweetness of the tender flesh below it. And he still craved more. More of the tastes of her.

Using his teeth, he scraped her inner thigh and felt the strong muscles quiver in response. She planted her feet and arched, opening herself to him. And he slid in to feast on paradise.

With one part of his brain, he heard her whimpering,

then screaming and calling his name—over and over. He kept tasting her varying flavors, tangy, salty, suddenly sweet.

But when he reached one hand up to soothe and touch her cheek, Bella took his forefinger into her mouth and sucked hard. That erotic pull muffled her screams and sent electric jolts straight through him. He returned the jolt with one more quick tug of his lips on her center nub.

The climax ripped through her like a hot knife on warm butter. She dug her nails into his shoulders and then grabbed fistfuls of his hair.

Sobbing, she let each fantastic aftershock rock through her. She relished it. Gloried in her first real climax. Breathless power drove heat swarming over her body.

"Now, Cal. Please, now."

"Not yet." But he quickly dispensed with his jeans and bent to her again.

He couldn't get his fill. Every time he thought his urgent hunger would finish him off, he found something new about her to tantalize and keep him going. He soothed and kissed, let her breathing deepen and calm.

His own breathing was shallow and threatened to clog his lungs. There was more to her than even he'd dreamed. He flipped her on her stomach and cherished the curve of her waist, the roundness of her bottom. He dug his hands into the smooth silk of her hair and buried his nose in handfuls of the sweet-smelling strands.

He ran his hands over the golden satin of her skin. Smooth, slightly sweaty from the exertion of her climax, he bent his head to taste.

He felt the tremble and heard her moan. He reached underneath her body and splayed his hand flat against her belly. Fire and ice. She shivered. But her skin was so hot it burned his palm.

Cal knew when he turned her over he would find her panting. And he had to turn her. Had to see her eyes.

Before he moved, though, Bella eased over onto her back and looked up at him. Her breath came in raspy, short gasps. The glazed look in her eyes was unfocused and wild. She reached for him, ran her hands up and down his arms. Her hips bucked. She moaned, arching her back and spreading her legs wide.

"Bella, look at me," he whispered.

Her eyes widened and focused on his. That was all he could see. Her eyes, glinting black with passion and want.

He rose over her, holding back while a look of amazement, mixed with a tiny bit of fear, passed through her eyes. Cal almost crowed with male pride.

Here lay everything he'd ever needed. The thought caught him off guard, as he plunged into her. Then all thought shattered and fled while her body closed hot and tight around him.

She first rose to meet him, then fell back to the bed while the pounding of two bodies mating stirred the night air. He watched her smile with pleasure and captured that smile with his mouth on hers. Their breaths mixed as they linked together, moving beat for beat.

He felt her heart thundering under his and realized their two hearts were joined in time. The same as their bodies were one.

The tempo of their bodies picked up, and the pounding became slaps, ringing in the darkness. He reached

for her hands and linked hers with his while her hips
urged him on.

Cal felt it when the wave began to rumble through
her. Little spirals of internal pulses sucked at his body
as he rammed into hers. Her breathing stopped and he
knew she'd gotten caught up in the crest.

Feeling the explosion of volcanic heat crashing
against him, and seeing the glorious surrender to pleasure on her face, Cal let himself slip. His own explosion whooshed the breath right out of his lungs as he
collapsed down over her.

When Cal buried his face in her hair, she was lost.
The minute she took her first breath and reveled in the
feeling of his body on hers, she knew it was all over.
She would never in her lifetime get over him. There
would never be another man who could make her feel
such things.

How stupid was she? To throw herself into the fire
this way. To practically beg the man to break her heart.

Bella was hopelessly in love. She'd tried to deny it
for days now. Kept reminding herself he'd never mentioned a future for them. And he most certainly was a
ladies' man, after all. She knew, because he'd just
pleased this lady into losing her heart.

He placed a gentle kiss against her temple, and her
eyes grew dim and damp. She blinked back the tears.
Closed her eyes and willed away the pain.

"Bella...I..."

A shrill whistle sounded faintly through the darkness, bringing Cal's words to a sudden halt. Distantly
Bella thought of the bird of prey that must've made
that sound. Then she opened her eyes, but the room
still seemed darker than before.

She felt Cal move away from her to sit on the side of the bed. Trying to focus, she realized that clouds had obscured the moonlight, casting the cabin and its occupants into alternating dark shadows and eerie nothingness.

"Stupid. Stupid. Stupid," Cal mumbled.

Dios Mío, she thought. He'd already realized that he'd made a horrible mistake with her. Even though she'd just been through the most amazing experience of her life. Could he really have changed his mind so soon?

Seconds later she felt his body tense as he sat at the side of the bed, and a shiver of fear ran up her spine. "Cal, what…?"

"Shush. Don't talk. Just get dressed."

She could hear him as he picked up his jeans and slid into them.

"I'm going for the rifles and the phone." He stood and moved toward the kitchen. "Stay in this room. No matter what you hear. Keep still."

And then with a whisper of denim, she knew he was gone.

Nine

Cal silently cursed himself as he stole through the cabin, finding first his phone and then one of the rifles. He jammed on a pair of boots and moved to the front room.

He'd been rash enough to think bringing Bella out here would keep her safe. Wiping a hand across his eyes, he cursed once more. Damnation! He couldn't even keep her safe from himself.

How could he have been stupid enough to make love to Bella without protection? He'd been cautioning himself for days now not to get carried away with her. Instead, when she'd come to him, he'd turned into the same stupid ass he'd always been.

He'd lost it. Lost his control. Lost his mind.

He vowed to stick with his plan regardless of the strange craziness he felt when he was with Bella. He was chagrined to remember that he'd lost his edge when it came to Kaydie, too. All that enticing weakness just had to change—and change now.

Cal vowed to go back to racing and leave Kaydie on the ranch. And now he added leaving Bella behind as well. He had to go. Had to protect himself. A strong person didn't allow themselves to be sidetracked by love. Love hurt.

All the people he'd ever cared about disappeared from his life. And when they went they took a piece of his soul with them.

But Bella seemed so different than all the others. She was special. Phenomenal.

They were good together, too. He knew they'd be back in each other's arms soon. But the next time, he'd be more careful. She was bound to hurt him if he didn't start using his head…and protection.

It might be crazy. He couldn't really remember feeling this way before, but he'd thought he was destined to protect Bella. Protect her from everything.

So far, he hadn't done much of job of it. And now it was way past time for him to start acting like an intelligent human being.

Standing in the dark, beside the closed front door, Cal phoned Cinco. When his brother answered in a quiet whisper, Cal figured he'd awakened him.

"I need your help, Cinco," he said with his own hoarse whisper. "The *coyotes* have apparently found us, and I think they're about to rush the cabin."

"I think you're right, little brother."

Cal pulled the phone from his ear and stared at it for a second. What had he just said?

He whipped the phone back to his ear. "Cinco, what the hell…?"

"Gotcha covered, kid. When you left Abby's muttering about protecting Bella, it suddenly occurred to me that if the *coyotes* were smart enough to find a way through a Gentry Ranch fence, they might be smart enough to follow you two when you left Abby's.

"I've got the sheriff and about a dozen men with me," Cinco continued. "We're here, about a half mile away from the cabin, trying to figure out how many men they've got and just where each of them is hiding."

Thank the Lord. "I heard a whistle a little while ago."

"Yeah, we're on it. It was some kind of signal. It looks like they're about to make a move." Cinco paused. "Stay put, Cal. Lock yourself and Bella in and barricade the doors. This will all be over soon. We'll get them."

Cal heard a click and Cinco was cut off. "Wait... Damn it," he sputtered.

How the hell was he supposed to stay in this cabin cowering under the bed when at any moment a *coyote* could break through and get to Bella? And what if they knew Cinco and the sheriff were out there? One of the good guys might get hurt.

No way was he staying inside. He needed to be out with the action, keeping an eye on Bella from the outside.

But he didn't want to scare her to death. She'd been upset enough today when she learned all the migrants had been murdered. What could he tell her?

He quietly slipped back into Kaydie's bedroom. "Bella? Are you dressed?"

"Oh, Cal, thank goodness. Yes, I put on my jeans and boots. What's going on?"

Bella's eyes had grown accustomed to the dark, and

when she saw him standing in the doorway, she rushed to throw her arms around him. "Did I do something stupid, Cal? If I did, I'm sorry. I didn't mean to…"

"Quiet!" He pulled her arms away from his shoulders and put them at her sides. "You did nothing wrong. It's just…I thought I heard something outside…near where the horses are tied. I'm sure it's nothing, but I'm going out to check. It might be an animal or a rattler."

He sounded so distant, and almost angry. And considering everything they'd just done together, too. Her heart hurt. After trying to prepare herself for this, she'd thought she'd be ready. But she was wrong.

"I want you to lock and barricade the doors behind me," he demanded harshly. "Then stay in this room until you hear my voice at the door."

"Oh, but I could help," she pleaded. "I could quiet the horses for you."

"Uh…the floodlights don't reach that far. I'll probably have to shoot whatever it is, and I might accidently shoot you in the dark." He pulled back from her. "Come on. Lock the door behind me, keep the lights off, and don't panic if you hear shots."

She did as he'd asked and soon found herself sitting in the dark on the little bed where they had just made love. Well, no, maybe it wasn't love they'd made. Maybe it was just great sex—at least for Cal. For her…for her it was so much more.

He'd made her feel cherished, adored and powerful. He'd needed her, if only for a little while.

She sighed, then quieted to listen for any sounds from outside. Not able to hear anything from this little protected bedroom, Bella sneaked into the kitchen to stand at the window.

But she couldn't hear anything there, either. Listening hard, she tried to make out the normal sounds of the night. The crickets or the calls of the nighthawks as they flew over the range.

There was nothing. No sounds at all but the wind as it gently rustled through the leaves of the mesquite.

Then she heard the first noise, but in short order it became a commotion. It threw her for a second, but soon she realized what was going on. The animal that Cal had heard was after the chickens in the pen near the house, not the horses down by the creek.

It might be a fox or even a coyote. Mabel! As ornery as she was, Bella still wouldn't let anything happen to her.

She ran to the kitchen door, grabbing a broom as she went. No darn fox was going to mess with her chickens.

She threw open the door and reached outside to turn on the spotlights that Cinco had installed for her last week.

And things seemed to go nuts.

Shots rang out in the distance. In fact, it sounded like a whole army was at war on Gentry Ranch.

When her eyes became accustomed to the bright light, Bella quickly looked around. She saw a man dressed all in black with his back to her, tangled in chicken wire and pointing a rifle toward the trees.

A light glinted off something under the trees and she narrowed her eyes to see what the man was preparing to shoot. Immediately she discovered the light was moonlight bouncing off Cal's rifle as he took aim at something he'd spotted out there. And the crazy man in with the chickens was about to shoot at his back.

But he hadn't counted on Bella.

She never hesitated, but raised the broom in her hands and brought it down hard against the man's arms. The rifle bounced out of his hands and exploded, sending its shot wild.

The man staggered then turned on her.

Dios mio. It was one of the *coyotes* she'd seen shooting that man in Mexico.

His eyes were black, empty. But his mouth was screwed up with rage.

Bella froze. They'd found her. And Cal was out there helpless against them.

The *coyote* stumbled as he shook one foot free of the wire. She watched him stomp around on the ground, still trying to extricate the other foot. She stood and stared as if in some terrible nightmare.

Then out of her dreams, she could hear Cal calling to her. "Get in the house, Bella! Get away from the light and lock the damn door."

That got her attention. She dropped the broom and scooted back inside. The door was locked and bolted and she was back in the baby's room before she took her next breath.

She leaned against the closed door and prayed. Prayed for Cal. How would he manage if he was outnumbered?

If she knew where he kept the other rifles, maybe she could help him. On the other hand, she'd never fired a gun in her life. And she wasn't sure she'd be able to kill anyone, even if she knew how.

Bella heard a couple more distant gunshots and then there was quiet. She held her breath. Cal. She didn't mind dying if it was her time, but she'd give anything to make sure he was okay.

A man's voice sliced through the silence, calling out

to her. But it wasn't Cal's voice. She gave up a quick prayer to be forgiven for any sins and prepared herself to die.

"Bella! It's me, Cinco. Come open the door. It's all over."

She ran to the kitchen door and threw it open. The floodlight, directed at the chicken pen, was still burning, lighting up the entire yard. Cinco had turned to call out to someone as she'd opened the door.

"Cinco," she breathed. "Where is…?" Bella stopped midsentence because at that moment Cal came into view.

There were at least twenty men in or at the fringes of the cabin's yard. Some were on the ground, bleeding and moaning. Other men seemed to be herding a few of the *coyotes,* who were all dressed in black, into a central spot.

The pungent odor of gunsmoke filled the night air. In the background, Bella could hear trucks coming down the dirt road toward the cabin.

But through it all, she'd spotted Cal as he found her gaze from clear across the yard. She couldn't see any blood or injuries on his body. He quickly spoke to another man and then headed in her direction.

"I think we got 'em all, sugar," Cinco told her. "The sheriff will be moving them to jail in town shortly."

She'd been distracted watching her love walk toward her. "Got all of…who? The *coyotes?* How'd you know they'd be here? I don't understand any of this."

Cal appeared by her side and dragged her into his arms. "Thank God you're all right," he groaned as he closed his wide arms around her body and hugged tightly.

She buried her nose in the material of his shirt and took a deep breath. He was alive.

"You saved my life, sweetheart," Cal whispered into her hair. "I was trying to save yours, and you—" He choked on the rest of the words.

Bella squirmed out of his embrace and pulled back to look at him. "You knew they were out there and you didn't tell me? You didn't trust me to help you?" Her eyes were on fire and she was spitting mad.

Cinco backed up a step, and Cal wondered whether his knee was healed enough to run.

Instead of taking the coward's way, he fell back on his old charms and stood his ground, grinning at her. "Sorry, honey. I didn't realize you were such a sure shot with a broomstick. If I'd known, we could've saved ourselves a whole lot of trouble...and bullets."

Instead of laughing at him as he'd hoped, she bent to pick up the broom. Cal decided it was time to go help the sheriff with his prisoners.

The following day wore into late afternoon and Cal's body was dragging. But as he looked out the kitchen window at Bella feeding her chickens and repairing the wire, he marveled at how well she was holding up.

Last night she'd tended some of the injured men, she'd made coffee, and she'd insisted he put his knee up when he hadn't realized it was bothering him. Competent, compassionate...and spectacular. He was stunned at all the things his Bella could be.

But most of all, he couldn't stop thinking about the wild and amazing sex scene they'd created together the night before. He'd known that passion was there. Known it as sure as he knew his own past.

Even thinking about it now, nearly twenty-four hours

later, he found the pure, savage fervor still sent electric impulses to harden and embarrass him.

Bella finished with her hens and came inside the kitchen. "How's your knee? Are you hungry?" She opened the refrigerator door and stood studying its contents. "We have some leftovers. Want me to fix you something?"

Cal shook his head. He was hungry all right. Just not for food.

"I think you should rest a bit," he told her instead. "If you want to eat, I'll fix it."

He avoided touching her hair as she got herself a glass of water. "Ray called a while ago, honey. He's coming out later and wants to talk to us."

She put a hand on her hip and turned to face him. "Haven't we had enough of talking to the sheriff and the FBI agents?"

It was true, they'd spent all the daylight hours today answering questions. Bella had held up well. She'd never backed away from an uncomfortable question or lost her cool when the realization of how close they'd come to being murdered really hit home.

But she had to hold up a little longer. "Ray said he has some important news and some serious questions to ask. I think we'd better hear him out."

"Okay. I guess so." She returned to the refrigerator and pulled out an aluminum-foil covered plate. "Let's eat a little something now. After Ray leaves we'll probably be going to pick up Kaydie and won't have time."

With her hands full, Bella turned and smiled at him. "I'm sure you can't wait to get your daughter back in your arms." Her whole face beamed when she spoke about the baby.

He'd forgotten all about his child. Kaydie was safe

and with people who really loved her now. Why mess that up?

"No I don't think we'll be getting Kaydie," he told Bella. "She's fine where she is."

Bella set the plate down carefully on the counter and turned to him. "Do you mean because it'll be too late for her and we should wait to pick up Kaydie until tomorrow?"

He shook his head, worrying about what she was going to think of him when he said what he knew he must. "No. I mean that Kaydie is where she should be. With Cinco and Meredith. I've been hoping that they'd fall in love with her and be willing to take her in permanently. And I believe that's just what's happened."

"But..." Bella's eyes blinked back her confusion. "I don't understand. You'll walk away from Gentry Ranch when you are well...and leave your daughter behind?"

In an effort to appear casual, Cal shrugged a shoulder. "That's my plan."

He almost couldn't bear the hurt look that had crept across Bella's face. Turning his back to her, he fiddled with the salt and pepper shakers on the table.

"My life on the racing circuit doesn't really lend itself to children," he explained over his shoulder. "What with all that travel and long hours." He held his breath...waited.

Bella stepped beside him and put a hand on his arm, just as he'd pictured she would. "But Kaydie needs you. When you love someone, you make time for them. You rearrange your life if necessary."

Her fingers burned a blistering spot into his arm so he jerked it out of her grip. "Love is for fools," he spat out and turned his back.

He hadn't wanted to go into all this with her. He knew she'd never understand. No one would.

"You don't know what you're saying," she said to his back. "Maybe you don't want to give your love to any woman. I can understand that. But…you love your daughter. I know you do."

"No," he roared hoarsely as he spun to face her. "I can't love anyone. Never again." He slapped a hand down on the counter. "Just leave it be, will you?"

"Cal, please," she begged. "Help me understand." She put one hand to her heart and one across her stomach, as if she must be feeling a terrible ache.

Cal hadn't meant to cause her pain. He was in enough misery for both of them at the moment.

"Look." He tried to soften his tone, but found his voice raspy, cracked and rusty. "I loved my parents with my whole heart and soul. They were everything to me. When they disappeared…"

He swallowed the shaky pain. "You don't know what it's like to love and then have that love ripped away from you. It's the worst…"

"No, it's not the worst," she interrupted, shaking her head sadly. "What's worse is never having been loved in the first place."

Bella dropped her hands to her side. "You don't know how lucky you are. You had parents who wanted you, who loved you. You have wonderful memories of a happy childhood."

She needed to take a breath of fresh air. Wanted to go hide somewhere and weep with the pain of loving a man who couldn't even let himself love his own daughter.

"Just think about this, Cal," she said as she backed toward the door. "Kaydie loves you. What kind of memories is she going to have of her parents and child-hood?'' Bella put a trembling hand on the doorknob. ''How is your child going to feel about having a father walk away from her? Isn't that so much worse than knowing your parents would've stayed with you if only they could?''

Bella opened the door. ''I'll be back in a little while to pack. I'm going for a walk, then I'm going to ask Ray to help me find a way to stay in this country. But not on Gentry Ranch. You don't need me anymore.''

She kept her back turned to the pain and sorrow she'd seen in Cal's face. ''I thank you for everything you've done for me, Señor Gentry. But I'll be out of your way by tomorrow.''

How could she have been so wrong about him? Was it possible that he was nothing more than a ladies' man with no feelings after all? If he didn't love his daughter… No, that was just not right. She knew she'd seen love in his eyes when he looked at Kaydie.

The man was full of conflicts and contradictions. Bella didn't know what to say to help him. Didn't know how to protect her heart or assist him in finding his.

Shutting the door behind her, she quickly made her way out of the yard. Bella dashed into the trees right before the tears blurred her vision and her shaking legs gave out. She dropped to the ground in a miserable heap of watery self-pity and cried as she'd always lived—alone.

Back in control, Bella ushered Ray into the front room a couple of hours later. She'd managed to miss seeing Cal when she'd come back inside. He'd been closed up in his room, and though she was glad not to face him, she hoped he'd gotten some rest while she'd packed her few belongings.

If he was determined to leave Kaydie and go back to racing, he would need all his rest to keep up his strength. She just hoped that in time her heart would mend as well as his knee had.

"Is Cal around?" Ray asked as she showed him to the sofa.

"I'm right here." Cal appeared, fully dressed in clean clothes and looking bright and rested.

Bella's heart thumped at the sight of him. But she bit her lip and sat down quietly on the sofa next to Ray.

"The immediate danger is over for you two." Ray sat, hands clasped between his legs, his emotionless face a mask. "But there's more to this situation than is clear just yet."

Bella thought the older man looked as if he knew a secret, and she couldn't help but wonder what it might be. "Is there something we should know?"

Ray slid a curious look in Cal's direction before he drew his attention back to Bella—without really answering her question. "The FBI is convinced that someone on this side of the border has been helping the *coyotes*. In fact—" his lips turned down into a deep frown "—well, they're sure that the real head of this whole human smuggling ring has yet to be uncovered."

Her breath hitched in her chest. It hadn't occurred to her that there might still be danger for them. She glanced over to Cal and found him studying her with a deadly serious expression on his face.

Ray continued with his explanations. "We also have a problem with the governor's aide in Mexico...Dr. Domingo's brother, remember?"

She nodded her head but stayed quiet.

"He's demanding your return to Mexico, Bella. He had your ambassador make a formal protest to our State Department." Ray glanced quickly at Cal, then deliberately softened his look when he spoke to her again. "There's a lot hidden about this whole mess. The FBI knows things they're not telling. But they've said they believe your life would be in danger if you return to Mexico."

Ray's concern was clear. He reached out to take her hand. "The FBI can't force you stay in this country. You're not really under their jurisdiction, but…"

"My fiancée is staying right here on Gentry Ranch, Ray," Cal blurted out. "If we have to get married to make it all nice and legal and get them off her back, then so be it. You can arrange everything."

Bella's head jerked around in stunned amazement at Cal's words. "What? Fiancée? But…"

Ray barked out a laugh, but his face turned serious again when he spoke. "Cal may be right, dear. Marrying a U.S. citizen is sometimes the only way to stay in the country." He patted the back of her hand. "Do you want to stay in the U.S.? Would you consider becoming a citizen someday?"

She nodded, still too shocked to speak. Staying in the United States was what she'd been hoping for. She'd be safe here. There was nothing for her back in Mexico, anyway.

Bella looked over to the man she'd fallen in love with but had decided she would have to leave. His face was hard, impossible to read.

Why was Cal saying these things about marriage?

Was he just trying to be noble and pay her back because he thought she'd saved his life?

"Yes, I want to become an American," she whispered, still watching Cal's face. "Very much."

Ten

"**Y**ou said you wanted to stay." Cal reached for Bella the minute Ray excused himself for the night and left the cabin. "Does that mean you'll marry me?"

He couldn't bear not holding her in his arms, so he crushed her to him. She was still in danger. There were forces swirling around her that she didn't understand.

But Cal understood one thing. The minute he'd realized she was in trouble, he knew he didn't want to lose her. He couldn't let her return to Mexico—especially since her life was in danger there.

Cal buried his face in her hair while the scent of soap and spicy pepper drew him ever deeper into the fiery bonfire that was Bella. He wanted her close. He'd gotten accustomed to her being around.

More than that, he needed her. Needed her in his bed. And needed her in his life. To hell with his old plans.

He'd given it some thought this afternoon when she'd left him standing in the kitchen. Why couldn't she come with him when he went back on the racing circuit? She could help with his physical therapy. He'd buy a big motorcoach and they'd travel from racetrack to racetrack together.

It wouldn't be exactly the life he'd left behind. But Cal wasn't so sure he'd really cared much for that lonely life, anyway. With Bella by his side, he'd have the best of both worlds.

But at the moment she was too quiet. "Say you'll marry me, honey." With a great internal struggle, he pushed her back to arm's length so he could see her face.

"Why? Why do you want me to marry you?" she asked.

"It'll keep you in this country. And…" He wasn't sure what she wanted him to say, so he flashed her one of his infamous smiles. "And it'll be a lot of fun. Think of how it'll be. We can travel from party to party on the circuit. You can help me stay in racing shape and I'll show you what the bright lights of stardom are all about."

"Fun…stardom." Bella took a step back. "No, Cal, I won't marry you. I…thought you knew me better than that."

Bella was absolutely astonished that her broken heart could still be ripped into shreds. How did the man keep getting to her this way? She would've thought she couldn't be tempted by him after all they'd been through. But he'd never mentioned Kaydie. He'd never mentioned need.

And yet here she was, imagining a long life spent loving and being loved and needed in return. She had to get ahold of herself. Obviously, Cal wasn't that kind of man. And hadn't he told her earlier that love was for fools?

Well, he'd certainly been right. She felt like every bit the fool now. He didn't love her. With his knee healed and without Kaydie, he didn't even need her anymore.

"Thank you very much for the offer, but I'll ask Ray to figure out another way for me to stay in the country," she told him.

"But...but..." Cal stuttered.

He looked confused. Bella nearly laughed. She'd be willing to bet that this was the first time a woman had told him no. Poor Cal.

But he'd be over his disappointment in a few days. Bella, on the other hand, might never recover from the heartache she'd given herself by falling in love with another ladies' man who refused to give his heart.

Before he could say anything else that might tempt her to reconsider, she quickly added, "Do you think it's too late to go to the main house? I can't stay here tonight after everything that's happened, and...I want to see Kaydie."

As the morning sun began to spill over the horizon, Bella stood at the window of the guest room where she'd slept last night, staring out at the rays of rose and gold sweeping over the rolling Texas countryside. She wondered if it was too early to go to Kaydie's room.

A soft knock on her door drew her attention from the peaceful scene outside. "Come in."

"Morning." Meredith swept into the room, carrying Kaydie in her arms. "Someone wants to see you." She handed the baby over to Bella.

"Aye, *niña*," Bella cried as she hugged the little girl close. "Kaydie. Kaydie. Kaydie. I've missed you so much." *Dios* help her, she was thrilled to feel the baby back in her arms.

Kaydie squealed, laughed and patted Bella's cheek.

"We're glad you've come, Bella," Meredith said through a smile. "Things have been so hectic. But I need to get back in a plane this morning and help check the fence lines."

"Oh?" Bella was confused by the woman's meaning. "But what about the housekeeper? What was her name...Lupe? She takes care of Kaydie when you work, doesn't she?"

"Lupe would love to care for the baby, but she thinks she's grown too old to do it right," Meredith told her. "Her arthritic hips and poor eyesight keep her from doing much of anything except for cooking. That she could do blindfolded."

The look in Meredith's eyes suddenly changed and she became thoughtful and quiet. "I'm sorry I wasn't awake when you and Cal came in last night. When Cinco told me you were here, I thought you'd come to take care of Kaydie until the trouble's all over."

Bella shifted the baby to her hip. This woman had always been friendly and now seemed so concerned. Bella hoped it would be okay to talk frankly with her. She needed someone to turn to for advice and friendship.

"I wanted to continue being the baby's nanny, but Cal said..." She caught herself before she accidently said the wrong thing. She wasn't positive that Cal wanted his brother to know his full intentions just yet. .

Bella took the conversation in a different direction.

"Ray came over last night and asked me if I wanted to stay in this country."

"And do you?"

"Of course. But apparently I need a good reason to keep Mexico from demanding that I return." Bella's eyes burned, but she refused to give in to fear and longing right now. Maybe later.

"I thought if I had a permanent job as Kaydie's nanny and good references from the Gentrys, it would be reason enough to keep them from sending me back. What do you think?"

Meredith looked curious. "What did Cal have to say about this?"

"He asked me to marry him."

"So that's the answer to the problem, isn't it?" Meredith asked with a grin.

Bella sniffed once and squared her shoulders. "No. I refused him. Cal doesn't love me."

"But you love him. Right?"

"*Sí.* I do love him," she admitted. "But…but…he's determined not to need me…not to let me love him. His past stops him from loving anyone."

Going to sit on the edge of the bed, Meredith's expression turned thoughtful. "I've heard that sometimes love can grow after marriage. And besides, everyone has some issue from their past that keeps things from running smoothly. You're not afraid Cal would cheat on you, are you?"

Bella shook her head and kept the tears at bay. She knew Cal would never cheat once he made a commitment. He was definitely not that kind of man.

"But he has already married once without love," Bella objected. "I don't want him to think of me that way. And…I need to be needed."

Meredith reached over and put a gentle hand on her arm. "Are you sure you're being honest with yourself about how you feel?" Looking deep into Bella's eyes, she didn't wait long for an answer. "Love isn't always easy, sweetie. Sometimes you don't get everything the way you want it. I think you're so accustomed to giving that you're afraid to take what's being offered."

"I...don't know." Bella forced back the fears and tried to assure herself she knew her own heart.

Meredith stood to leave. "Well, you have the job as Kaydie's nanny for now...if that helps any. You can stay here on Gentry Ranch as long as you want. Cinco and Ray will see to it the Mexican government leaves you alone."

Bella hugged Kaydie to her breast after Meredith left to go to work. "Oh, Kaydie. I know you would grow to love me. I'd never leave you. And if I got the chance, I'd always be there to care about you."

She couldn't imagine risking her heart with a man who wouldn't take a chance on love, though. Instead, she would learn to be content with friends and a child who really needed her.

Bella had never known what being loved was all about. Perhaps this baby was the chance she'd been seeking. Going off with a man whose past kept him from needing her or his child would be just too scary to contemplate.

Cal eased out of the cab of a Gentry Ranch truck and balanced himself on his good leg. It had been an interesting morning.

He'd wangled himself an invitation to sit in on one part of the FBI's interrogation of the *coyotes*. That was all he could think to do that would seem useful. He wanted to help keep Bella safe.

And ever since she'd turned down his marriage proposal last night, he'd been trying to get his head on straight where she was concerned. He'd thought about losing her. About attempting to make a life without her in it.

And he knew he couldn't. She'd done something to his soul. Opened a locked gate he'd forgotten all about. There would be no going back.

He wasn't positive yet what it would take to make her want to keep him around. But he intended to stay by her side for the rest of their lives. Somehow.

As Cal walked toward the kitchen door leading into the house where he'd been raised, he marveled at some of the things the *coyote* had told them about Bella. It seemed that she'd become a legend among the shadowy people trying to cross the border.

The *coyotes* considered her a meddling saint. They claimed she could talk anyone into changing plans, no matter how desperate they might've been in the beginning. The stories about her had grown to nearly epic proportions.

She was an advocate for the downtrodden, who were exactly the people the *coyotes* preyed upon. The human smugglers feared her power and imagined that God shielded her from harm.

Have mercy, but Cal burned with need for her.

He stepped through the door at the main house and his heart stopped. Bella sat on the kitchen floor trying to coax Kaydie into standing on her own. It was a normal, peaceful family portrait but something about the scene opened another gate inside him.

Bella had been right when she'd said that abandoning his child would be worse than what his parents had done. He had a choice—they hadn't.

Looking down at his precious baby, so happy and so beautiful, he realized now that nothing would make him leave her behind. He didn't need parties and late nights on the circuit. He needed his little girl.

And he needed Bella to make the family picture complete.

"Hello, Cal." She turned to look up at him.

Kaydie spotted him then and her face lit up. "Da!" She raised her arms and bounced on wobbly knees.

Cal's knees were every bit as wobbly as his daughter's. "Did she just call me Dad?" He reached down and picked her up, cradling her close.

"Maybe." Bella smiled, but her eyes looked a little watery. "Or maybe that was just baby talk. Either way, I know she's glad to see her papa."

Nuzzling Kaydie's hair, Cal watched as Bella got to her feet. He had to find a way to get her to marry him.

He'd decided to try using his old charms. And he didn't mind trying to use her feelings for his daughter, either. But before anything else, he certainly planned to use the sexual pull between them to convince her to stay with him.

Anything. Anything at all to make her say yes.

"You missed the noonday dinner." Bella went to the refrigerator. "But Lupe left you a plate. Shall I heat it up for you?"

He laid a hand on her arm, keeping her from opening the door. "No thanks, honey. I'm not hungry. I had a bite to eat in town with the sheriff." He hated the stiffness between them and vowed to put an end to it soon.

She took her hand from the door handle and casually tugged her arm loose from his grip. "Did the authorities learn anything useful today?'' Bella looked over at Kaydie and didn't meet his gaze.

''Yeah, they've learned a few things. Uh…is Meredith back from making her rounds? I'd like to talk to you. And I want you to come with me.'' He tried to look sober and sincere when she finally glanced his way. ''I thought maybe Meredith would watch the baby for a couple of hours.''

Bella's eyes widened and she tilted her head to study him. ''Your sister-in-law is working in her office. She's had a crib installed there for Kaydie, so I imagine she wouldn't mind keeping an eye on her while she takes a nap.''

It didn't take much convincing to get Meredith to agree to watch Kaydie. And it didn't take Cal long to hustle Bella into a jacket and out the door.

The clear, crisp autumn afternoon sun lay light as a cloud against the empty barnyards and corrals near the main house. The hands were out working on the range, while the rest of the animals rested in their stalls or pastures on other parts of the ranch. What a marvelous day for getting engaged.

''Where are we going, Cal?'' Bella looked confused, but he could still see the trust in her eyes.

''I thought you'd like to come along while I pick up the laying hens from the cabin.'' He took a long breath and chided himself for using every trick he could think of. But when the prize was Bella, he didn't care about playing fair.

Her face brightened. ''Goodness, I almost forgot about the chickens. I hope they're all right.''

''They're fine.'' He grinned and slipped an arm around her waist. ''Cinco sent a couple of wranglers out to pick up the mares this morning. I thought you'd rather be the one to put the hens into their cages for the ride back.''

"Oh, yes. Mabel would not like anyone else to touch her." Bella's mood lifted at the thought of going back to the cabin.

This afternoon might turn out to be fun. Cal was being his old charming self. He looked marvelous in his dress jeans and plaid long-sleeved shirt. But then, his looks had always been spectacular as far as Bella was concerned. This afternoon he looked good enough to make any woman faint.

Cal helped her into the truck's cab and then climbed into the driver's seat. He'd had to put his hands around her waist to lift her into the passenger seat, and Bella's heart thumped wildly in her chest at his nearness.

As hurt as she'd been at knowing he didn't need her or Kaydie, she still wanted him. It seemed rather traitorous of her body to react to him this way, she thought briefly. But sitting here next to him, she knew if she had half a chance, they'd be back in each other's arms.

Even if it was only to say goodbye.

"What's in that pretty head of yours all of sudden?" he asked as he started the engine and pulled out of the yard.

His voice sounded gentle and concerned. Just like he'd been so tender and loving with Kaydie today. Bella couldn't imagine how he could be that way and still want to leave that sweet baby on the Gentry Ranch when he left.

She'd realized that she didn't want to ever leave the little girl. If there was a way, Bella intended to help raise that child. Kaydie would always know that someone cared about her.

"Oh, Cal. I almost slipped and told Meredith you'd

be leaving Kaydie with them when you left to go back to racing. Have you told your brother your intentions yet?''

He reached over and put a hand on her shoulder. ''That's one of the things I wanted to talk to you about.''

Bella caught him sliding a wary glance in her direction. But his voice stayed even and he appeared to be casual and relaxed as he continued to concentrate on the road ahead.

''I've changed my mind, honey. Or maybe it's that I've come to my senses.'' He pulled his hand back to the steering wheel, while his mouth turned up in an odd smile. ''I was stupid not to realize I couldn't walk away from my own daughter. I have you to thank for making me see that.''

''You mean this?'' she gasped. ''You really intend to take Kaydie with you when you go back to racing?''

He nodded. ''Sure. Just like you said. I need Kaydie and she needs me.''

Bella couldn't find her voice, couldn't really get a grasp on the huge change in his plans. Her head suddenly hurt, and the flash of panic came quickly. What would that mean for her relationship with Kaydie?

She'd already turned his marriage proposal down flat. And she didn't have the nerve to go back on all she'd said. He'd laugh at her for begging and then walk away.

But Cal just couldn't take Kaydie from her now that she'd decided not to leave the child. It would be too cruel.

Bella suddenly came to a life-changing decision. She'd find a way to get him to take her along with them as the baby's nanny.

As they pulled up under the trees in the cabin's yard, she wondered what it would take to get Cal to agree with her plan. Hmm. Would he want her around even if he couldn't have her?

Cal got out of the truck and came around to open her door, but she slid down on her own and was waiting for him when he got there. He hadn't worn a hat today and the sunlight made the reddish highlights in his hair look the color of rusty pennies. The way he was looking at her made her impossibly hot.

The tingles began in her fingers as he took her elbow and lead her into the cabin. Convincing him would not be any hardship, she'd decided.

Bella pulled off her jacket and gazed around the cabin as if it hadn't been just yesterday that she'd last seen it. She really loved this little house. She'd been so happy for the last month that she'd lived here. Actually, happier than she could ever remember being before.

She spun around in a circle, taking it all in. "We left everything so clean. It looks wonderful."

Cal chuckled at how very alive she was. "You'd never have left last night if we hadn't washed down every speck." He wanted to keep her inside for just a little longer, until he had a chance to tell her the rest of his plans. "Did you leave anything behind that you might want to take with you?"

She turned to him and smiled, standing there in the patch of hazy sunshine filtering through her sparkling clean windows. Bella was simply the most beautiful— and absolutely the sexiest woman he'd ever beheld. A few strands of her hair had been tousled by the wind and her skin was flushed with emotions.

His vision blurred for a second. He'd been blinded

by the expression of utter need he'd glimpsed on her face. But when he focused again, she was laughing as she twirled around the room.

"No, I did not forget anything." She pulled the ribbon from her hair and shook back her head. Her hair looked like a soft black shawl as it spread out over her shoulders.

"You look so handsome today," she said as she waltzed over to him. "I must tell you about the dream I had of you last night."

She put her hands on his chest and stood on tiptoe to place a kiss on his cheek. He automatically reached for her, but she spun just out of reach.

"I…" He'd lost his voice, and he struggled to give her the space she apparently needed.

"It's very warm in here, don't you think?" she asked. "Will we be here long enough to open the windows?" She fanned herself with her hand and then undid the top button on her blouse.

"Uh. Open the windows if you want." His throat was hoarse. His mind was blanking out again.

At this moment he wanted her more than he had wanted anyone or anything in his entire lifetime. She was so perfect. He tried to tell himself to go slow but it was useless. Deep inside, his heart wanted to believe she'd never hurt him—never leave him.

"Oh, I wore too many clothes for such a warm day." She rolled up her long sleeves and wiped up a drop of sweat as it trickled down her neck.

The sight of her touching her own body made his blood pressure go through the roof. He took a step in her direction.

"You don't have to keep your shirt on if you're too

warm in here,'' he gulped. ''It's just us. I've seen you without a shirt before.''

Bella chuckled and slowly undid the rest of the buttons on her shirt. One at a time. The material inched apart, exposing the honey-colored swells of her breasts peeking over her white bra.

He swore under his breath and reached for her once more.

Laughing, Bella slipped away from his fingers and dropped her blouse on the floor. ''You mustn't touch me, Cal. I want to be the one. It's my turn.'' Kicking free of her shoes, she unzipped her jeans and quickly shucked them.

''Yeah?'' He saw the mischief in her eyes…and the raw passion. ''Whatever turns you on, babe.''

''Good,'' she said and picked up his hand. ''I want you to be crazy for me. I want you to want me so much that you beg.'' She lifted his hand and pressed it against her heart. ''I want you, Cal. Feel my heart beating fast for you?''

He sucked in a gasp as she placed her own hand over his, trapping both on her breast.

It was like taking the fourth corner on the last lap of a five-hundred-mile race, he thought. Staring into those deep brown eyes was like winning the cup. She took his breath away, shot adrenaline to every inch of his body, and caused his temperature to rise to the boiling point.

He couldn't have answered her if his life depended on it. Everything else faded away but his darling Bella.

Her eyes widened and darkened when she finally settled her gaze on his. ''Uh…don't you want to hear about my dream?'' She raised her chin and combed back her hair with her fingers.

Without a word, he grabbed her up, plundering her mouth and claiming the sizzle of heat and joy that she yielded. As he pulled her to the floor, her laugh sent pleasure through every pulsating nerve in his body.

Eleven

—

"**O**h no, you don't," Bella said, giggling.

She rolled on top and straddled him. "I want to do the things to you that I did in my dream." Her eyes were nearly black with passion as she licked her lips.

"Have mercy on me, Bella, please?" Cal was too ripe with need for her.

"I do intend to please you," she laughed.

He clamped down on his desire as she reached behind her, undoing her bra. Slowly she drew it aside, revealing full breasts and hardened tips.

Biting back the rush, he vowed not to hurry her. His hands slid up her torso, cupping her breasts. She filled his palms. Hot, bursting with pleasure, smooth as glass.

She lowered her lips to his, but lingered a half inch away. "No hands, remember?" she whispered.

When he dropped them to the floor, her lips brushed his. Teasing, nibbling, nipping. He groaned and she changed the tone. Angling her mouth across his, she pillaged with an intensity that spoke of her urgent wants.

He punched his fists against the rug. Every muscle in his body ached with the strain of holding back.

"Good. That's good," she mumbled. "I want you to beg."

She placed quick, greedy bites down his neck and found his nipples. Sucking. Licking. Kissing lower still.

She reached for his waistband, undid the button and took her time lowering the zipper. He was being destroyed, slowly but surely. He lifted his hips when she tugged against the denim, and she slid his jeans off and pitched them aside.

When his hands came up to grip her hips, she batted them away. "No. My turn," she murmured and reached for his shaft. The gleam in her eyes changed to self-indulgence.

Cal took in the scent of her—mixed with sweat, stirred with lust. He'd never had a woman take him before. But Bella was certainly taking everything he had.

Her hair spilled over both of them and added to the erotic sensations that were slowly killing him.

When she clamped her mouth over him, sucking deeply, he bucked under her and fisted his hands in her hair. The sensations caused chaos in his body. Every quaking, quivering muscle screamed that he'd just run out of patience.

With his hands still gripping her hair, he dragged her head back to see the dark burn in her eyes. "Enough!"

"Beg," she panted.

He ripped her panties off with one forceful swipe. "I need you," he growled. "Now! I'm begging you."

She helped him when he lifted her hips this time. Then he drove himself into her warmth and wetness. Bella cried out as completion came quickly, surprising both of them.

Throwing her head back, she screamed. "More," she shuddered, arching against him.

Cal reached one hand down between them and pushed her over the edge once again. The speed and violence which rocked her body as she climaxed a second time shoved him past all good reason. He pumped his seed into her while a rain of sensations jolted through them both.

She collapsed down on top of him, and he marveled as the aftershocks rippled through her. He locked his arms around her and waited for his head to clear.

Bella's body felt weightless. Numbed, but wallowing in the internal pleasures of Cal, she realized she'd gotten what she'd wanted. He'd said he needed her.

He pressed a kiss to her hair, murmuring about how wonderful she'd made him feel. And she felt the tears backing up behind her closed eyelids. It wasn't enough.

Who would've guessed? Fantastic sex. Tender moments. They weren't nearly enough.

Cal had finally admitted that he needed her, but he hadn't said he loved her. He was everything to her and she wanted to be everything to him in return. She managed to swallow past the lump in her throat and wondered how she'd come to be so greedy.

Rolling out of his embrace, Bella drove her hands through her hair, pushing back the wild strands so she could study him clearly. Cal opened his eyes, and she saw him trying to focus on her face.

He reached out for her. "I need you desperately,"

he whispered. "Marry me, Bella. Come away with me and Kaydie when we leave. Take care of us."

Shaking her head, Bella backed away from him. "I can't marry you, Cal. I can't put myself through that much pain."

She grabbed her clothes, stood and gazed down on him. "I want very much to continue being Kaydie's nanny. So I intend to consider going with you to care for your child. But I won't be your wife…or your lover."

"Bella," Cal began as he stood up. "I don't understand. What we have is so good. Better than good. And you want me—I know you do. I feel it every time you look at me."

Turning her back to him, Bella stepped into her jeans and slipped them over her hips. "The sex is the best of a lifetime," she admitted. "But it's not enough."

"I need you. What more do you want?"

"I'm sorry. I can't explain it. I just know I want more…I deserve more." She fled into the bathroom before the flood of tears threatened to drown them both.

Bella still felt weak and weepy several hours after they'd returned the hens to the main ranch. On the way back and all through the dinner meal, Cal sat stone-faced. She hadn't had any clue that loving someone this much could hurt so deeply.

It was getting late when Cal stuck his head through the kitchen door. She'd just finished drying the last dish that Meredith washed and handed to her. "Can you two come into Cinco's office for a few minutes?"

"Sure," Meredith answered, and dried her hands. "What's going on?"

"We've got Ray on the speakerphone in there," Cal

told her. "And he wants Bella to hear something. Then he has something to say to all of us."

Bella reluctantly followed them through the house, wondering what the family attorney might have to say to her. Cinco showed her to the chair next to his desk when they arrived at his office. Meanwhile, Meredith and Cal arranged themselves on the couch.

Bella took her place and listened to Ray over the speakerphone. "Sit tight a minute, Bella," he said. "I have someone here in the office and I want you to listen to him speak."

The next thing she heard was the man's voice that had plagued her nightmares for over a month. Bella put her hand over her mouth to keep from screaming.

"I don't know what you want me to say," the dreaded male voice roared in protest to an unheard command. "What?" A muffled conversation took place at the other end of the line.

"Fine. Whatever." The mumbling out-of-body male voice on the phone changed languages. *"Jésus Cristo. Encuentre esa mujer,"* he muttered in a deliberately flat tone.

Bella gasped and put her hand to her throat. *Find that woman!* It was the man she'd heard that night, right before she'd slipped out of the truck with the migrants. He'd been the one giving orders to the *coyotes.*

Cal saw Bella's face pale. And he was out of his seat, kneeling by her side before he could blink. Slipping his arm around her, he threw a wicked glare over his shoulder at Cinco while trying to find the words to comfort his Bella.

"Easy there, darlin'," he murmured in her ear. "It's

just a voice on the phone. He can't hurt you. You're safe.''

She was trembling and breathing hard. Cal couldn't stand to see her like this. His proud, strong Bella was reduced to a whimpering mass of nerves.

He hated it. Hated seeing her so vulnerable. But at the moment she needed his help. Needed him.

That last thought seemed like an important change. But he ignored it for the moment as he barked out orders to his brother and sister-in-law.

Meredith scurried to bring Bella a glass of water. While Cinco snatched up the phone and growled out a few choice orders of his own.

Cal used his thumb to wipe away the tears that streamed down Bella cheeks. "It's okay," he murmured over and over.

A few minutes later her breathing had evened out and Cal began to relax. The golden color was returning to her face, and her eyes no longer held that frightened-deer look.

"Ray has to ask you a question, sugar," Cinco said quietly. "Can you answer him now?"

Bella scooted to the edge of her chair and nodded.

Cal's heart was so full of her, he thought he'd burst. He placed a firm hand on her shoulder to give her strength.

"I take it you've heard that voice before, Bella," Ray said over the speakerphone. "That was Dr. Domingo. Is he the man you told the FBI about? The one whose face you never saw, but who you overheard issuing orders to the *coyotes?*''

"Yes," she replied. "That is the same voice I heard.''

"Thank God," Ray murmured. "After all this time. It's finally over."

Cal was curious when he heard the very real relief in the family attorney's voice. The old friend of the Gentry family seemed unusually emotional about the FBI making a case against their suspect. He started to ask why it concerned Ray so much. But before he could say anything, Ray's voice came through the speaker once again.

"The FBI has been trying to make a case against Dr. Joe Domingo for years. They knew he led a large ring of alien smugglers, but they didn't have enough evidence."

Ray's voice grew more determined. "Two of the *coyotes* we captured named him as their boss. In fact, they've implicated his Mexican-national brother in an even bigger operation then just human smuggling.

"Their gang has been into drugs, gunrunning and slavery. Nasty stuff. The Mexican police have arrested the brother. And the Justice Department intends to request extradition to the U.S."

Ray cleared his throat, while Cal tried to take it all in. "Bella, your testimony is the last piece of corroboration they needed to charge Domingo with ordering the murder of those Mexican migrants," the elder man told her. "He'll be facing the death penalty."

Ray's voice grew tentative once more. "Better yet, he and his brother will be off the streets and rendered impotent…at last."

"Ray," Cal interrupted. "We need more information. What else is going on?"

The elder man gave him an easy laugh. "I don't have time to go into it at the moment. But believe me, the Gentry family has reason to celebrate with Bella."

A muffled sound cut off his words for a second. "Right. I have to get off the phone now. But I'll be out tomorrow night with the whole story. Make sure Abby and Gray are there. I'll be around after supper." With that, the phone went dead.

Cal hadn't felt much like celebrating. Oh, he'd been relieved that all of the danger surrounding Bella was gone. But he was troubled by the fact that now it was over and he was well again, it was time for him to leave the ranch.

He'd been planning for this time and reaching for his old life for so long that he knew he should feel ecstatic. But he wasn't. What he still felt was confusion about what Bella wanted. About how to convince her to marry him.

She'd said she would consider coming along with him to be Kaydie's nanny. Well, if that was all he could get at first, he'd take it. But he would never give up on getting her to say yes to marriage. He had to be sure she'd be with him always.

Cinco brought out a bottle of wine to celebrate, but Bella declined the offer and went upstairs to check on Kaydie. Cal figured this was a good time for him to go to Abby and Gray's ranch. He needed to get out of the house for a little while to think.

By tomorrow night he'd have to find the key to Bella's heart. Or he'd be forced to accept her terms and agree to having her be merely the baby's nanny. He was positive that would ultimately be an intolerable situation for everyone.

What did she really want? And more—what was he really lacking? Sighing heavily, he walked out into the cold, dark night.

* * *

For the entire next day, Bella was groggy and tired. Something was wrong with her body. She'd never slept this much, cried this much or felt so weak in her entire lifetime.

Tonight she'd helped with the big family supper and then put Kaydie to bed before it was time for Ray to come by with his news. Cal hadn't said more than two words to her since he'd walked in the door with Abby and Gray.

Bella wondered if he'd changed his mind. Things were too confusing. All she knew for sure was that she loved both Kaydie and Cal. But knowing that meant she would also very likely get hurt in the end.

She came down the back stairs just as Lupe let Ray into the kitchen from the outside. It seemed late. The dishes were all put away. The overhead lights had been dimmed, and the night was black and starless against the windows.

Bella held back outside the kitchen doorway as Ray came into the room. Neither Lupe nor Ray spotted her there.

"Well, Lupe, my old friend," Ray said as he tugged at his coat. "It's all over. Are you ready to face the ending? I'm shaking like a leaf, myself."

Lupe narrowed her eyes. "We did what we had to do." She crossed her arms over her chest. "They're good children…loving adults. They will understand."

"I'm most worried about Cal," Ray told her. "He's never made peace with himself. He's always been a hothead. Still…" Ray turned to throw his coat over a chair and saw Bella hesitating in the doorway.

"Oh, hi, Bella." He brightened. "Is everything ready for our family meeting?"

She was curious and guilty about being so nosy, but

she managed to keep her questions and feelings inside. "*Sí.* Everyone is in the great room in front of the fire, waiting for you. Uh…except Kaydie. I put her to bed."

Ray waved a hand in front of his face. "Oh, that's fine. We can get her up when we need to."

What an odd thing to say. Bella's curiosity grew.

Ray walked to her side and slipped her arm through his. "After this is all over, I have something to talk to you about, Bella. I've been thinking about ways for you to stay in this country, and I've talked to several people. I believe I've come up with a terrific idea."

He guided her down the hall to the great room as Lupe followed behind. "Um…you'd better sit beside me, young lady," Ray whispered as they entered the room. "Things might get a little intense."

After Ray pointed Bella to a small sofa, he went to stand in front of the fire. He looked as if he was ready for a speech—and maybe a fight.

Bella braced her hands against her seat and let her gaze wander over the others in the room. Cinco sat on the other long sofa with his arm around Meredith. They looked so content with each other that tears filled her eyes.

Abby sat in an overstuffed chair, looking as curious as Bella felt. Her husband stood behind her chair with a protective hand lying lightly on his young wife's shoulder. Gray's face held his usual wary expression. You could tell he'd be ready to kill anyone who tried to hurt Abby.

Cal sat stiff and upright in a straight-backed chair next to the fireplace. He'd thrown a curious glance at Bella as she and Ray entered the room, but he sat quietly, waiting for Ray to begin. Lupe took her place behind him.

"First of all," Ray said. "I'd like for all of you to keep an open mind...and an open heart...until you've heard everything tonight."

He sent a pointed stare Cal's way, and Bella wished she could move closer to the man she loved. She had a feeling he was going to need her strength tonight. But Ray had already begun and it was too late.

"I have a long story to tell you," Ray said slowly.

"Just say what you came to say and get it over with," Cal muttered.

That brought a smile to Ray's lips. "I'm afraid you're going to have to sit through this whole thing, Cal. It's important for you to hear it all."

Ray shifted, then began. "Uh...once upon a time..."

"Oh, brother," Cal groaned.

"There was a happy family," Ray continued as if he hadn't been interrupted. "A mom and dad and three kids all lived on a big Texas ranch. Everything was great until one day the mom and dad flew off on a short vacation to go hunting at their lodge in Mexico."

Bella watched as the whole room sat up in their seats and stared quietly at Ray.

"Their small plane developed engine trouble and they had to land a few miles short, on a neighboring ranch's airstrip in Mexico. To make a very long story a little shorter, the mom and dad discovered there was a gang of international thugs using the neighbor's ranch as a hideout. They saw drugs being readied for transport...bound and gagged young women being pushed into vans...and crates full of rifles and ammunition sitting in a hidden warehouse."

Ray stopped to swallow against an obviously dry throat. The room was hushed. No sounds dared to break the stillness—except for the crackling fire at Ray's back.

"Well," he began again. "They spotted a powerful Mexican official as his limo drove into the compound. They knew who he was. Knew about his connections in the U.S. But unfortunately, he'd spotted them, too."

Bella glanced quickly around the room. Cinco had leaned forward, his eyes narrowed and dark. Abby's eyes were wide and she looked frightened. Cal had slouched down in his hard chair and his eyes were closed as if he was taking a nap.

Bella knew Cal was awake. Knew he was listening carefully. But the man she loved seemed to be trying to protect himself by pretending not to care. It was a revelation.

"Well, the mom and dad made it back to the U.S. and went straightaway to the authorities." Ray kept on with his story. "But within a few days, they began to receive threats and warnings. At first they thought they could protect themselves against the danger, but soon the warnings centered on their children. It was too big a risk for them to take.

"The FBI wanted their testimony but they didn't have enough evidence to make any arrests. They offered to put the family into a protection program and hide them away until they could fully investigate and convince the Mexican government to cooperate on wiping out the gang."

A log broke in the flames and crashed against the grate. Ray stopped for a second and took a breath before continuing.

"One huge problem with the offer of protection for the family centered around the children," he told them. "Five was too large a group to hide together. The authorities wanted the family to spilt up. Two children with one parent, one with the other. But one of the kids had already gone off to college. His parents couldn't ask him to totally change his life and hide indefinitely.

"And leaving him behind alone was out of the question. If the gang thought he knew where they'd gone, he'd be in the ultimate danger. So the mom and dad agonized for a week over what to do. Finally it was decided that they would go into the protection program by themselves. They would pretend to be killed to throw off the bad guys. Leave all their children at home…ignorant of the dangers…and with the family housekeeper and their best friend to care for them."

Chaos erupted in the room. Abby gasped and jammed her fist against her mouth, while Gray came around the chair to pull her into his arms. Cinco fisted his hands but hung his head, shaking it sadly as Meredith spoke softly in his ear.

Cal jumped up, grabbing the front of Ray's shirt. "Where the hell are they? Are they alive? Tell me!"

"We're alive, son." A tall older man quietly entered the back of the room, but spoke forcefully to be heard over the noise. "And we have been in hell. But we're home at last."

Every head in the room turned to him, gaping in silence.

An elegant-looking, gray-haired woman stepped out from behind the man, tears streaming down her cheeks. "We're so sorry for the lies and the pain, my darlin's. But we thought…thought it was for the best. We were positive the most important thing was keeping you children alive. We never realized how hard…how many years…how much pain…"

"Mommy! Oh, God, Mommy. It's really you."

Abby tore out of Gray's grasp and ran to her mother's waiting arms.

The elder Gentry hesitated a second, then moved toward his sons. Cinco stood, stunned and disbelieving, and waited for his father while Meredith kept hold of his hand. But Cal growled low in his throat, then stormed from the room.

"Cal!" Bella jumped up and started after him.

"Give him a few minutes to himself." Cal's father held up his hand to stop her. "It's a lot to absorb at one time. I'll go to him after a while. As soon as he cools off."

Bella watched the reunions swirling around her, but her heart ached for Cal. After Ray introduced her to Cal's parents, she sneaked upstairs to sit quietly in Kaydie's room.

She knew Cal needed her right now, but she couldn't think of a way to help him. And what's more, she was sure he wouldn't let her into his heart.

More frustrated and confused than ever, Bella lightly put a hand on Kaydie's fuzzy head and let the tears fall.

After thirty-six hours of no sleep, Cal's body had begun to droop. Groggy and tired, he sat alone on the hillside where his parents' empty graves had languished for the past thirteen years. The late-afternoon sun threw lengthening shadows against the mesquite and cottonwood, and cast the headstones into a gray shade.

Incredibly, he wasn't angry. In fact, after the first flash of temper last night, Cal had begun to think clearly for the first time since he'd been a kid.

He turned his head as the sound of a truck making

its way up the hillside pierced the silent scene. When
the engine died, his father climbed down out of the
cab, nodded in Cal's direction and made his way to the
bed of the truck.

Cal got to his feet and went to see what he was
doing. "What's up...Dad?"

T. A. Gentry jerked his head around and smiled. "I
can't tell you how it makes me feel to hear someone
call me that again after all these years." He reached
into the truckbed and pulled out a pick and shovel.
"I'm going to dig up your mother's and my grave-
stones. Want to help?"

For the first time in days, Cal broke out in a smile.
How fitting, he thought. The only thing that might've
been better would be digging new graves for Joe Domingo and his brother. But his mother, father and Bella
would be doing about the same thing with their testi-
monies—and that was almost as good.

The two generations of Gentrys set to work destroy-
ing the marble monuments. After a moment's struggle
with himself, Cal spoke first. "Dad, do you remember
the last time we talked before you...?"

"Uh...disappeared," T.A. supplied. "It's been a
long time. What'd we talk about?" He took another
swing, and the crack of breaking marble filled the autumn air. The remnants of so many hurt lives crumbled
to dust.

"We had an argument," Cal told him. "I wanted to
try racing full-time, and you wanted me to get a college
education first." He leaned on the shovel. "I was so
mad at you. I wished you'd just disappear from my
life."

Cal's dad looked up and shook his head. "Son, I'm
sorry. The guilt you must have carried all this time. I

was so sure what we were doing was right. I didn't stop to think about all the consequences.''

T.A. swiped a hand across his eyes. ''I remember thinking that your real calling was to be a lawyer. To go into politics. You'd been dreaming about that for such a long time. I guess I didn't realize how much you'd come to love driving too.'' He cleared his throat and put a hand on Cal's shoulder. ''But, son, you have to see that I would've never left you behind if I'd known how much you'd be hurt by it. My heart breaks when I think of what you've been through.''

A third gate finally opened in Cal's heart. ''I, uh, think I want to stay on the Gentry, Dad. I want to raise my daughter here. I talked to Cinco this morning about moving into Granddad Teddy's little cabin permanently. Bella has helped me see that I still love this ranch. I belong here.''

''That's a right smart little gal, that Bella. Pretty too.'' T.A. grinned. ''She reminds me of your mom back when she was letting me think I was chasing her. And she seems to love my granddaughter too. That makes her real intelligent in my book. You say she likes it here on the Gentry? Then where's she rushing off to? I'd have thought you'd want to keep that one roped down.''

''Rushing off? Leaving?'' Cal choked. He hadn't talked to her since last night, but he'd been soothed by thinking she was safe at the ranch and taking care of Kaydie—waiting for him. The fear and panic smacked him hard in the gut.

''Yep. Cinco helped her down the stairs with a suitcase. And I believe it was Ray she drove away with.''

''How long ago?'' Cal was already out of breath and hadn't moved yet.

"'Bout twenty minutes, I'd say. Didn't you know she…''

Cal jumped into the Suburban, slammed the door and cranked the engine. "Dad, I can't lose her. I've got to go. We'll talk more later. Leave the rubble of the headstones. I'd just love to be the one to shovel off those old nightmares." He put the truck in gear. "Maybe I can catch Bella before they reach the main gate. I need her, Dad. Wish me luck."

Bella heard a horn honking from behind their car and saw Ray's surprised look when he glanced in the rear-view mirror. He shook his head and pulled over to a stop. Before she could ask a question, her passenger door had been yanked open and Cal was glaring down at her.

"Were you just going to leave with no explanation?" Cal snapped. "With no goodbye?"

Ray leaned over so he could see him and spoke quietly. "We're just headed to my house in town, Cal. She'd have called you later."

"Shut up, Ray. And stay put." Cal reached around her and undid her seat belt. "Get out, Bella. We need to talk."

Cal looked angry. She'd been positive that she was doing the right thing by leaving. It never occurred to her that it might make him mad. She slid out of her seat and stood on wobbly feet beside him.

"Let's walk," he demanded as he grabbed her elbow and stormed up the shoulder of the road. A tense silence surrounded them as he dragged her about twenty feet away.

"Cal, please don't make a scene," she begged. "Once you think about it, you'll realize this is for the best. Cinco told me about you not going back to racing and wanting to stay on the ranch. You won't need me for that.''

She planted her feet and stopped. ''And Kaydie has a grandma now to care for her. She won't need me anymore.''

''Stop it.'' Cal took hold of her shoulders and turned her to face him. ''Look at me.''

She didn't want to look at him. The hurt of knowing he didn't need her anymore was too fresh. ''You don't have to worry about me. Ray's found a way for me to go to law school on a grant and with your government's blessing. I have to agree to do three years' advocacy work for undocumented migrants when I get my degree and my citizenship. But that'll be no hardship. I'd—''

''Bella, my love, please look at me.''

She knew she'd been babbling, and Bella hadn't wanted this goodbye to drag out. But what had he just called her?

When she finally raised her eyes to meet his, all she could see was his heart, blazing through gray-green pupils. Her own heart lurched and thumped in her chest.

''Bella,'' he whispered roughly. ''Forget about whether we need you or not. What's in your heart? Do you love me?''

He was talking about the same thing she'd realized on her own several days ago. She might as well admit the truth. He'd probably never want to see her again, anyway.

''All right, Cal. It's true. I have let myself depend on you and Kaydie—too much. All this talk about you two needing me was just a way to cover up that I was the one who needed you."

Bending, he claimed her mouth with a sizzling kiss. When they finally came up for air, he smiled at her. "Damn it, woman," he grinned. "You're going to force me into telling you everything, aren't you?"

He took a step back. "I didn't want to need you or Kaydie. I had wished for my parents to disappear, and they were gone. Then when Jasmine and I fought bitterly in the car that day over her seeing another guy, I wished she was out of my life...and she died instantly."

Taking a long breath, he continued. "I was petrified of getting too close to anyone else. I knew I was a jinx. A bad seed that could wish people dead."

"Oh, Cal. No. You're not..."

Abruptly, he dropped his arms to his sides and Bella wanted to pull him back into an embrace. She wanted to give him comfort, and fought to think of the right thing to say.

"I know," he mumbled. "It was stupid and childish. You've made me see that." He shook his head and grimaced.

"Bella..." Cal was the one who reached out for her now, and she stepped closer. "You are my soul...my everything. Say you'll stay on the Gentry with us. I love you more than I ever thought possible. But for God's sake, put me out of my misery and please tell me you love me, too."

Her breath hitched in her throat, but she managed to whisper the words that would change three lives forever.

"I love you, Cal. And I'll stay. For always and ever."

Epilogue

Cal ripped off the maddening tie and unbuttoned his top button. Taking a huge breath, he relaxed and gazed around. The puffy white clouds in the crystal-blue sky seemed quite appropriate on this his wedding day.

And what a great day it had been. The first Thanksgiving in thirteen years that the entire Gentry clan had been together, and it seemed like the whole county had come to celebrate. They'd had three weddings in one year on this ranch, but his had been the best. His mother and father had made it so.

"Congratulations, son." Kay Gentry drifted over to him with a champagne glass in her hand. "I couldn't be more pleased with your choice."

Cal felt the grin spread out across his face, as he reached around behind him and dragged his new bride to his side. "Thanks. Tell her that."

His mother laughed and hugged Bella. But his darling wife had a question to ask her new mother-in-law.

"Señora Gentry…Kay. I still don't understand something. Why couldn't you have told your children that you had to go away? Why let them think you were dead?"

"Mostly it was because of Abby. She was too young to understand the danger. The FBI was afraid one of the kids would slip and mention that we were alive. Dr. Domingo knew everything that happened in this county. He would've heard, and they would've found us." Kay's eyes filled with regret. "I've cursed that decision a thousand times since."

Cal threw an arm around his mother's shoulder. "Don't think about it. This is a day for happiness. We have so much good news." He smiled over at Bella. "I've decided to run for the vacant office of county judge, Mom. I think Castillo County could use a new point of view."

"I'd say you're right," Kay brightened. "That's even more great news. I'd been thrilled enough to find out Abby and Gray are expecting my second grandchild. And with you two happily married now…"

"And expecting your third grandchild," Cal interrupted with a proud smile.

"What? How wonderful!" Kay began to cry and hugged him. "I love you both so much."

And with his family here and his new bride by his side, Cal knew he'd finally figured out how to accept that love.

*   *   *   *   *

Silhouette®

Desire

is proud to present
an exciting new miniseries from

KATHIE DeNOSKY

Lonetree Ranchers

On the Lonetree Ranch, passions explode
under Western skies for these
handsome-but-hard-to-tame bachelors.

In August 2003—
LONETREE RANCHERS: BRANT

In October 2003—
LONETREE RANCHERS: MORGAN

In December 2003—
LONETREE RANCHERS: COLT

Available at your favorite retail outlet.

Silhouette®

Where love comes alive™

COMING NEXT MONTH

#1525 THE LIBRARIAN'S PASSIONATE KNIGHT—
Cindy Gerard
Dynasties: The Barones
Love was the last thing on Daniel Barone's mind…until he rescued
Phoebe Richards from her pushy ex one fateful night. The shy librarian
was undeniably appealing, with her delectable curves and soft brown eyes, but
had this sexy bachelor finally met the woman who'd tame his playboy heart?

#1526 BILLIONAIRE BACHELORS: GRAY—
Anne Marie Winston
After Gray MacInnes underwent a heart transplant, he began having
flashes of strange memories…which led him to his donor's elegant widow,
Catherine Thorne, and her adorable son. His memories of endless nights
with her in his arms soon became a breathtaking reality, but Gray only
hoped Catherine would forgive him once she learned his true identity.

#1527 THE HEART OF A STRANGER—Sheri WhiteFeather
Lone Star Country Club
When she found a handsome stranger unconscious on her ranch,
Lourdes Quinterez had no idea her life was about to change forever.
She nursed the man back to health only to learn he had amnesia. Though
Juan Guapo, as she called him, turned out to be Ricky Mercado, former
mob boss, Lourdes would stand by the man who'd melted her heart with his
smoldering kisses.

#1528 LONETREE RANCHERS: BRANT—Kathie DeNosky
Never able to resist a woman in need, bullfighter Brant Wakefield was happy
to help lovely heiress Annie Devereaux when she needed protection from a
dangerous suitor. But soon they were falling head over heels for each other, and
though Brant feared they were too different to make it work, his passion for her
would not be denied.…

#1529 DESERT WARRIOR—Nalini Singh
Family pressure had forced Mina Coleridge to reject her soul mate four
years ago. Now circumstances had brought Tariq Zamanat back to her—as
her husband! Though he shared his body with her, his heart was considered
off-limits. But Mina had lost Tariq once before, and *this* time she was
determined to hold on to her beloved sheik.

#1530 HAVING THE TYCOON'S BABY—Anna DePalo
The Baby Bank
All Liz Donovan needed to realize her dream of having a baby was a trip
to the fertility clinic. But then the unthinkable happened—her teenage crush,
millionaire Quentin Whittaker, proposed a marriage of convenience! It wasn't
long before Liz was wondering if making a baby the old-fashioned way could
lead to the family of her dreams.

SDCNM0703